'So,' Vito was saying, and his Italian accent was doing wonderful things to her, as well as what his warm, admiring eyes were doing, 'am I to call you only *bella signorina*? Though if I do,' he murmured, his lashes sweeping over his eyes as his gaze dipped to meet hers, 'it would be nothing but the truth. *Bellissima signorina...*'

She took a breath. The air seemed to have too much oxygen in it suddenly. 'It's Eloise,' she said. 'Eloise Dean.'

He smiled again, warm and intimate, and she felt breathless.

'Come,' he said, and there was that low husk in his voice again, 'lean on me, Signorina Eloise Dean. I'll take care of you.'

She gazed up at him. He seemed very tall, she realised. And absolutely devastating... Her breath caught, her lips parting softly, and her eyes were wide as she just stared up at him, drinking him in.

The sculpted mouth quirked again. Long lashes swept down over deep, dark eyes.

'Oh, yes,' he said softly, 'I'll take care of you...'

From Mistress to Wife

From the bedroom—to the altar!

Eloise and Carla have never expected irresistible
passion—until they meet the powerful alpha
billionaires who will steal their innocence. But nights
of passion can have unexpected consequences...

When Eloise Dean falls at Vito Viscari's feet,
they are both overcome with a desire
they can neither resist or deny!

Claiming His Scandalous Love-Child

Available now

Carla Charteris knows falling for the enigmatic
Count of Mantegna will only bring heartache, but
what will happen when temptation proves irresistible?

Carrying His Scandalous Heir

Coming soon

You won't want to miss this passionately sexy duet
from Julia James!

CLAIMING HIS SCANDALOUS LOVE-CHILD

BY
JULIA JAMES

First Published in Great Britain 2017
By Mills & Boon, an imprint of HarperCollins*Publishers*
1 London Bridge Street, London, SE1 9GF

© 2017 Julia James

ISBN: 978-0-263-07006-4

MIX
Paper from
responsible sources
FSC™ C007454

This book is produced from independently certified FSC paper
to ensure responsible forest management. For more information
visit www.harpercollins.co.uk/green.

Printed and bound in Great Britain
by CPI Group (UK) Ltd, Croydon, CR0 4YY

Julia James lives in England and adores the peaceful verdant countryside and the wild shores of Cornwall. She also loves the Mediterranean—so rich in myth and history, with its sunbaked landscapes and olive groves, ancient ruins and azure seas. 'The perfect setting for romance!' she says. 'Rivalled only by the lush tropical heat of the Caribbean—palms swaying by a silver sand beach lapped by turquoise waters... What more could lovers want?'

Books by Julia James

Mills & Boon Modern Romance

A Cinderella for the Greek
A Tycoon to Be Reckoned With
Captivated by the Greek
The Forbidden Touch of Sanguardo
Securing the Greek's Legacy
Painted the Other Woman
The Dark Side of Desire
From Dirt to Diamonds
Forbidden or For Bedding?
Penniless and Purchased
The Greek's Million-Dollar Baby Bargain
Greek Tycoon, Waitress Wife

Visit the Author Profile page at millsandboon.co.uk for more titles.

For Pippa—thank you for all your hard work!!

CHAPTER ONE

THE SONOROUS MUSIC SWELLED, lifting upwards to one last crescendo before falling silent. The hushed murmurings of the congregation stilled as the priest raised his hands and began to speak the words of the ancient sacrament in the age-old ceremony.

Inside his breast Vito could feel his heart beating strongly. Emotion filled him, and he turned his head towards the woman now standing at his side.

Gowned in white, her face veiled, his bride waited for him. Waited for him to say the words that would unite them in marriage...

Eloise sipped her champagne, her eyes drifting around the gilded *salon privée* of the hotel, one of the most famous on the Promenade des Anglais in Nice on the Cote D'Azur in the South of France.

The *salon* was crowded with women in jewels and evening gowns, men sleek in tuxedos. But Eloise knew with absolute conviction that no other man present could possibly compare with the man she was with. For he was, quite simply, the most devastatingly handsome male she had ever seen in her life, and her pulse quickened every time she looked at him. As she did now.

Her eyes returned to his tall, distinctive form, so superbly sheathed in a hand-tailored tux, his sculpted Roman profile and the sable hair that moulded his well-shaped head. Her gaze caressed the smooth, tanned skin, taut over high cheekbones and chiselled jawline, the ready smile of his mobile mouth as he chatted in French—which he spoke as well as he did English and his native Italian—to the others in their little group. She felt her stomach give its familiar little skip.

Is this really me, being here like this? Or am I dreaming it?

Sometimes she thought it must be the latter, for the past weeks had been a headlong, heady whirl in the arms of the man at her side now, at whose feet she had, quite literally, fallen.

Memory, warm and vivid, leapt in her consciousness...

She had been hurrying along the airport concourse towards her departure gate, where her flight was already closing. It was her first holiday for ages, snatched before she knuckled down to look for a new placement as a nanny. Her most recent post had come to an end when the twins she'd been looking after had started school.

They would miss her for a bit, but they would soon adjust to her absence, Eloise thought—just as she herself had coped with a succession of nannies and au pairs in her own childhood. Her mother had not just been a mother with a busy job, but one supremely lacking in maternal feelings, and Eloise had long had to acknowledge this—just as she'd had to acknowledge that, because she'd been born a girl, her father— faced with her mother's adamant refusal to have any more children—had abandoned them both to seek a new wife who would give him the sons he craved.

Eloise's mouth tightened in a familiar fashion at the thought of her father rejecting her for his new family, playing no further part in her childhood.

Is that why I became a nanny? Eloise sometimes wondered. *To give warmth and affection to children who don't see much of their parents? Like me?*

She certainly loved her job—even though her mother had never been able to understand it. Just as she couldn't understand why her daughter would have preferred her father to stay in her life. Her mother's views were simple—and stark.

'Fathers aren't in the least necessary, Eloise. Women are perfectly capable of single motherhood! And it's just as well. Men let you down—far better never to depend on them. Far better to raise a child on your own!'

Eloise had refrained from pointing out that actually she had been raised by nannies, not by her mother...

But I'm not going to be like that—and I won't pick a man who'll desert me, either!

No, her life would be very different from her mother's—she was determined on it. She would prove her mother completely wrong. She would fall deeply in love with a wonderful man who would never leave her, never let her down, never abandon her for another woman, and never reject their children, whom they would raise together in loving devotion.

Just who that man would be, she had no idea. Oh, at twenty-six she'd had her share of boyfriends—she knew without vanity that her blonde good-looks had always drawn male attention—but none had touched her emotionally. Not yet...

But I'll find him, I know I will! The man I'm dreaming of! The man I'm going to fall in love with! It will happen one day.

But as she'd raced onward to the closing gate that day, she had been fine with being footloose and fancy-free, ready for a good holiday, travelling as lightly and comfortably as she could, wearing jeans, a T-shirt and casual jacket, and well-worn pumps.

The shoes must have been a tad *too* well worn, for suddenly, without warning, she'd skidded, her foot shooting sideways. She had gone careering down in a heap on the hard floor, her pull-along cabin bag slewing in the other direction, slamming into the legs of another passenger. She'd heard a short, sharp expletive in a foreign language, but had paid it no attention. Pain had been shooting up her sprawled legs, and she'd given a cry.

'Are you all right?'

The accented voice had had a low, attractive husk to it. But as Eloise had lifted her head, still feeling the sting of pain from her fall, her line of sight had impacted with a crouched pair of very male trouser legs, the fine light grey material straining over hard-muscled thighs.

She'd lifted her gaze further up. And the breath had just stopped in her throat. She'd stared. She'd been able to do nothing else.

A pair of dark, deep eyes fringed with inky lashes had looked at her with an expression of concern. 'Are you hurt?'

She'd tried to speak, but her mouth had suddenly been completely dry.

'I...' she croaked. 'I'm...fine.'

She started to get up, but a pair of strong hands was lifting her to her feet with a strength that made her seem completely weightless. But then, gravity seemed to have disappeared already. She had the strangest feeling that she was floating two inches off the ground.

People were walking and hurrying and talking all around them, but it was as though they didn't exist. She just went on staring helplessly at the man she had knocked into.

'Are you sure you are all right? Would you like me to summon medical assistance?'

There was still the same warm concern in his voice,

but it had a hint of humour in it, too, as though he were well aware of how she was staring.

And why...

A slanting smile sifted across his face. Eloise felt her insides go hollow. The thickly lashed dark eyes washed over her, and the hollowness increased a thousandfold.

'I believe this is your bag,' he said, and stooped to rescue her carry-on.

'Thank you...' Eloise answered faintly.

'My pleasure.'

He smiled again. He didn't seem to mind that she was still gazing at him, drinking in his dark, expressive eyes, his sable hair, the sculpted mouth with its slanting smile, the cheekbones that seemed to be cut from the finest marble.

She swallowed. Something was happening and she was reeling from it. And it had nothing whatsoever to do with having just tumbled down at his feet, or her luggage slamming into his legs.

Realisation hit. 'Are *you* all right?' she exclaimed, contrition filling her voice. 'My bag thumped right into you!'

He waved a hand dismissively. '*Niente*—it was nothing,' he assured her.

With the fragment of her brain that was still functioning Eloise registered that he spoke in Italian—then simultaneously registered that his gaze was as focused on her as hers was on him. She saw his eyes narrow minutely, as though studying her in great detail. Studying her and finding that she was entirely to his liking...

She felt colour run up into her cheeks, and as it did so she saw a glint spark in his gorgeous dark eyes. It was a subtle message between them that only heightened her colour and made her suddenly, piercingly, aware of her body and its reaction to being looked at with such intensity.

Oh, my God, what is happening?

Because never, *never* had she felt such an immediate overpowering response to a man. She gave a silent gulp of awareness. He was speaking again, and she dragged her fragmenting mind to order.

'Tell me, which gate are you heading for?'

Belatedly Eloise recalled what had been uppermost in her head until a few moments ago. Her eyes shot to the display by the gate further down the concourse, which now read, 'Flight Closed'.

'Oh, no!' she said with a wail. 'I've missed my flight!'

'Where were you travelling to?' he asked her.

'Paris...' she answered distractedly.

Something flickered in the man's eyes. Then, in a smooth voice, he said, 'What an extraordinary coincidence. I'm on my way to Paris myself.'

Was there the slightest hesitation in his voice as he named his destination? She had no time to think as he continued to speak.

'Since it was my fault you missed your flight, you must allow me to take you there myself.'

She stared, her mouth opening and then closing like a fish. A fish that was being scooped up, effortlessly, by someone who was—and the fact came to her belatedly— a very, very accomplished fisherman.

'I couldn't possibly—' she began.

The dark, beautifully arched eyebrows above the dark, deep eyes rose. 'Why not?' he said.

'Because—' She stopped.

'Because we don't know each other?' he challenged, again with that querying lift of his brows. Then his slanting smile slashed across his features. 'But that is easily remedied.'

His mouth quirked, making her stomach give a little flip.

'My name is Vito Viscari, and I am entirely at your service, *signorina*—having caused you to miss your flight.'

'But you didn't,' Eloise protested. '*I* did. I skidded. Crashed my bag into you.'

He lifted his free hand dismissively. 'We have already agreed that that is of no account,' he said airily. 'But what *is* of account is finding a medic to check your foot. There's plenty of time before our Paris flight leaves.'

Eloise looked at him dazedly. 'But I can't just swap flights—my ticket won't let me.'

The amused look came again. 'But mine will. Do not worry.' He paused a moment, then said, 'I have frequent flyer miles to use up. If I don't use them they'll be wasted.'

Eloise looked at him. Whatever else there was about him, he was not someone who looked as if he gave the slightest consideration to something as money-saving as air miles. Everything about him, she registered, from the tailored suit that fitted his lean body like a hand-made glove, to the gleaming black hand-stitched shoes and the monogrammed leather briefcase he was carrying told her that.

But he was talking again as he helped her forward. Looking down at her with that warm, admiring look in his eyes that made her forget everything except the quickening of her pulse, the heady airiness in her head.

'So,' he was saying, and his Italian accent was doing wonderful things to her, as well as the effect his warm, admiring eyes was having on her, 'am I to call you only *bella signorina*? Though if I do,' he murmured, his lashes sweeping over his eyes as his gaze dipped to meet hers, 'it would be nothing but the truth. *Bellissima signorina...*'

She took a breath. The air seemed to have too much oxygen in it suddenly. 'It's Eloise,' she said. 'Eloise Dean.'

He smiled again, warm and intimate, and she felt breathless.

'Come,' he said again, and there was that low husk in

his voice again, 'lean on me, Signorina Eloise Dean. I'll take care of you.'

She gazed up at him. He seemed very tall, she realised. And absolutely devastating...

Her breath caught, her lips parting softly, her eyes wide as she just stared up at him, drinking him in. The sculpted mouth quirked again. Long lashes swept down over deep dark eyes.

'Oh, yes,' he said softly, 'I'll take care of you...'

And Vito Viscari had done just that ever since. It had only been much later that Eloise had learnt that Vito hadn't been travelling to Paris at all. He'd been heading for Brussels. He'd swapped his destination to Paris for one reason and one reason only, he'd openly admitted to her, with a caressing, bone-melting smile. To woo her. And win her.

And he had succeeded. Succeeded quite effortlessly.

She hadn't put up even a token reluctance at being wooed and won by Vito Viscari. In fact, Eloise thought with rueful admission, she had participated in the process with every sign that being whisked away to Paris and romanced in the most romantic city in the world by the most gorgeous, devastating man she had ever met was in the nature of a dream come true!

And it still felt that way all these weeks later. Weeks that had passed in a complete haze, her feet hardly touching the ground, as Vito had whisked her across Europe from one luxurious hotel to another—each and every one a Viscari Hotel, one of the world's great hotel chains, owned by his family.

He had told her he was making an inspection of all his European hotels, of which it seemed there were a great many, situated in Europe's most beautiful, vibrant and historic cities from Lisbon to St Petersburg. And as Eloise had travelled with him, cocooned in a haze of romantic bliss, all thoughts of returning to the UK to start work again had begun to fade. How could she think of giving up Vito? Being with him was as intoxicating as champagne.

Yes, but even champagne runs out in the end—and in the end we always wake from our dreams...

That was what she had to make herself remember.

Now, as she stood beside him in this glittering environment of luxury hotels and high society, she could hear that voice inside her head. For, however intoxicatingly romantic it had been to waft across Europe in Vito's arms, feeling herself headily on the brink of something she had never before felt for a man, there were still questions she could not blind herself to.

Can I trust my own feelings? How real are they? And what does he feel for me?

Oh, he desired her—there was no doubt about that, no doubt at all! But was that *all* he felt? Certainly now, as he glanced down at her, she saw the warm glint in his eyes and knew that desire was real, burningly real—in her, as well as in him. Desire such as she'd never felt before for a man.

'Eloise?'

Vito's voice, his soft, oh-so-sexy Italian accent that always made her breath catch, set aside her thoughts.

'They're serving supper—let's go through.'

Together they walked into the adjoining *salon*, where a lavish buffet supper had been laid out. A woman glided up to Vito—a few years older than Eloise, more Vito's age, immaculately gowned in a clinging designer number in blonde satin that matched the pale blonde of her hair. It was their hostess, holding this evening party at the Viscari Nice to which, of course, Vito had been invited.

It had not taken Eloise long to realise that Vito moved in high society circles—not just in Rome, but in all the sophisticated, cosmopolitan places where rich people gathered. His looks, his wealth, his background all made him a favourite—as did his bachelor status. That last, she was only too aware, drew women to him like moths to a flame. Including, so it seemed, their hostess tonight.

'Vito—*cherie*! How lovely that you're here for my little party! I must drag you away some time to talk over old times together!'

The woman's wide smile passed from Vito to flicker over Eloise. The pale blue eyes glittered with a hint of frost.

'So, you are our gorgeous Vito's latest, are you? *How* he loves beautiful blondes!'

She gave a tinkling laugh, and glided off.

Vito looked down at Eloise, a rueful expression in his eyes. *'Mi dispiace,'* he said. 'Stephanie was quite some time ago—long gone, I promise you!'

Eloise smiled forgivingly. It didn't bother her, and nor did any of the attention that other women lavished on Vito. Oh, he was charming and polite to all of them, but Eloise knew that the sensual glint of desire in his eyes was for her and her alone.

But will it last? Being the woman in Vito's life?

An invisible tremor went through her. One day would she be the next Stephanie? The next beautiful blonde ex?

Or was something else growing between them? Something that would mean much more to both of them? *Could* there be?

Again, the questions hovered in her mind. Seeking answers that it was too soon for her to give. Reminding her of the need for caution where her heart was concerned.

Hadn't her mother fallen head over heels in love, committed herself in marriage on a whirlwind of romance, only to find out too late how deeply incompatible she and her husband were on matters that were of profound importance to them both? A discovery that had torn them apart and lost their daughter her father.

I mustn't make the same mistake. It would be so easy to tell myself I'm in love with Vito! Especially when I'm living this kind of dream existence...one gorgeous hotel after another!

But his European tour would be completed soon, for it was all part of Vito making his mark in his new role as head of Viscari Hotels. It was a role he'd been jettisoned into at the young age of only thirty-one, after the unexpected death of his father.

'I've had to step into large shoes,' he'd told Eloise, his face shadowed. 'I'm the only Viscari left—the only one to carry on the legacy. It all rests on me now. I can't let my father down.'

Had there been a tension in his voice that was more than grief for his lost father? But all he had gone on to say was how Viscari Hotels had been founded by his great-grandfather, the redoubtable Ettore Viscari, at the end of the nineteenth century, during the heyday of luxury hotels. He had then passed it on to his son, and thence to his two grandsons—Vito's father, Enrico, and Vito's childless uncle Guido.

It had been Guido who'd overseen a major expansion of the chain across the globe, as more and more international locations had become fashionable destinations for the rich clientele the hotels catered to.

Now, as the fourth generation of the Viscari family, it was clear to Eloise, that Vito was pressingly conscious of the legacy he had been left to run, and of the demands it made on him—including much of his social life, as it was this evening and all the evenings since she'd been with him.

'All this socialising with people who are or who will be guests at the hotels is unavoidable,' he said now. 'But, however wearing it gets, I can never let it show.' The shadows had left Vito's face. 'Your being with me makes it so much less onerous!'

It lifted her heart to hear him say such things, and she felt a familiar little thrill go through her—a thrill that was accentuated when, as he helped her to a plate of delicious food, she saw a telltale glint in Vito's dark, lustrous eyes.

Soon—oh, very soon—he would murmur his farewells to their hostess for the evening, take his leave of the other guests smoothly, courteously, and then whisk Eloise away to his suite to have her entirely to himself! To indulge in a night of exquisite, sensual bliss...

A tremor of anticipation went through her. Making love with Vito was like nothing she had ever known! His skilled, sensitive touch could bring her to an ecstasy that left her breathless, took her soaring into a stratosphere she had never known existed—and that seemed to sweep away all her questions and wariness about her headlong romance with him.

As she lay in his arms later, her heart beating like a wild bird, she felt emotion pour through her. Felt full of longing...

Oh, Vito—be the one for me! Be the one man for me!

It was so easy—so dangerously easy—to believe that he was that one man she could love.

But dare I believe it? Dare I?

She could not answer—only knew in those moments that above all else she longed to dare. Longed to believe he was the man for her. Longed to let herself love him.

CHAPTER TWO

VITO EASED THE throttle and settled down into a cruising speed along the *autostrada*. They'd just passed the Franco-Italian border at Mentone and were heading to his next stop, the Viscari San Remo, along the Riviera dei Fiori.

It had been a crowded morning, meeting with his managers at the Monte Carlo Viscari, outlining his strategy, addressing their specific issues, taking in their input and feedback. That had been followed by a working lunch, and only now, in mid-afternoon, were they travelling on. Heading back into Italy.

He was filled with mixed emotions. It was good to be back in his homeland after weeks out of the country, that was for certain, and yet he was all too aware that his extensive European tour—necessary though it had been— had been something he'd welcomed for quite different reasons than simply to make his mark as the new head of the company with his management teams.

It had got him out of Rome. Given him a lengthy break away from the city and the complications that it contained. Complications he could well do without.

Automatically, his mouth tightened. Those complications still awaited him, and in a couple of days they would be in the forefront of his life again. Somehow he would have to deal with them.

But not yet.

Deliberately, he shook them from his thoughts. No need to spoil these last few carefree days—not when he had Eloise at his side.

Eloise! He turned to glance at her, and as his eyes lit briefly on her beautiful profile he felt his spirits lighten. How totally and absolutely glad he was to have followed through on that first overpowering instinct that had speared him as he'd raised her to her feet from the concourse at Heathrow airport.

Of course it had been her glowing blonde beauty that had first captivated him—how could he possibly have resisted such a gift! He'd always had a passion for blondes, ever since he'd been a teenager, first discovering the enticements of the opposite sex, and as he'd looked down at the gorgeous, long-legged, golden-haired beauty who'd been gazing up at him with celestial blue eyes out of a face that was as gorgeous as the rest of her, he'd been instantly smitten.

The immediate desire he'd felt for her then had been richly fulfilled in Paris, and it had seemed the most natural thing in the world to continue his European tour with her at his side. With every new destination he'd reaffirmed how right he'd been. For it was clear to him that it was not merely Eloise's stunning looks that were so captivating. Unlike so many of his previous *inamoratas*—the elegant Stephanie in Nice, for example—Eloise was possessed of a sweetness of nature he had not encountered before. She was never capricious, never demanding, never out of temper. Her sunny mood seemed constant, and she was always willing and complaisant, easy-going and smiling, happy to do whatever he wanted to do.

He had never known another woman like her.

His eyes went back to the road ahead. There was a slight question in his expression now. In a couple of days they'd be in Rome.

Will we still be together?

Or would it be time to end their affair? In his many previous love affairs it had always been he who'd moved on, bidding his lover a graceful farewell before waiting for the next beautiful blonde to cross his path and catch his interest. He'd enjoyed every affair, had been faithful and attentive during the course of each one, but when he'd ended them he'd had no regrets about knowing it had run its course.

A frown shadowed his eyes. Would it always be like that? One easy affair after another? Until—

Until what? What is it that I want?

It wasn't a question he'd ever posed to himself so insistently. Yet he knew the answer to it all the same. Maybe he'd always known it.

I want to find a woman I can love as deeply as my father loved my mother!

That, he knew, was what had always been his goal. But was it attainable?

Maybe that's why I play the field—because I don't want to be disappointed in love. I fear the impossibility of making a marriage that was as happy as my parents' marriage.

A shaft of sadness went through him. Yes, his parents had been supremely happy together, and he, their only child, had had the benefit of it—had been adored by both of them. Now there was a rueful expression in his eyes. Maybe even a little spoilt.

But Vito knew that knowing he was the apple of his parents' eyes had also made him supremely conscious of his sense of responsibility towards them—to be worthy of their devoted love for him. That shaft of sadness came again…and something more. Since his father's untimely death life had not been easy—not for his stricken mother. Her widowing had been cruel indeed, and Vito knew that the haunted look of grief in her eyes would never leave her.

But maybe when I marry—give her a grandchild? Then she might be happy again!

Who would be his bride, though? Again, his eyes flickered to Eloise, his expression questioning.

What is she to me—and what do I want her to be? Could she truly be the woman who will come to mean everything to me?

He did not know and could not tell. Not yet. Not until they reached Rome and there was an end to this constant travelling. For now, he would just continue to enjoy their time together.

'Did you know,' he said smiling, 'that San Remo is renowned for its flower market? And that every year the city sends its finest blooms to Vienna, to adorn the annual New Year's Day concert?'

'How lovely!' Eloise's smile was as warm as ever. 'I've always adored watching that concert on TV. All those Strauss waltzes! And I'll never forget the night we spent in Vienna!' Her smile widened. 'Tell me more about San Remo,' she invited.

With her cerulean blue eyes fixed smilingly upon him, Vito was only too happy to oblige.

Their stay in San Remo was fleeting, and soon they were driving on towards Genoa, before turning south towards Portofino, and then the pretty villages of the Cinque Terre and the Tuscan coastline. Rome was only a day away now.

As they neared the city Eloise could feel her mood changing. These last few days with Vito it seemed her ardency in his passionate embrace had been even more intense than ever. She had clung to him as if she would never let him go.

But I don't want to let him go! I don't want this to end. I want to stay with him.

That was the emotion that was distilling within her as every passing kilometre brought them nearer to Rome. And when they finally entered the city, as she watched Vito tangling with its infamous traffic with long familiarity, she could feel that emotion intensifying.

Will he take me to his apartment? she wondered, as they drove into the Centro Storico, where all Rome's most famous landmarks and sights were.

But she realised they were pulling up outside the Viscari Roma—the original Viscari Hotel. Vito was telling her about its history, and she could hear the pride in his voice as he did so—could see how eagerly he was greeted as they made their way towards an elevator that whisked them up to what had originally been the attics, now redesigned as a penthouse suite.

Eloise let Vito lead her out on to a little roof terrace, gazing out at the city beyond.

'Roma!' He sighed, sliding an arm around her waist and pointing out the famous landmarks that could be glimpsed, and the outline of the fabled seven hills—they looked low, to Eloise's eyes, but she marked them fondly all the same, for they were dear to Vito.

And he is dear to me.

The thought was clear in her head, catching at her consciousness. Making her lean into him even more, wrap her arm around his strong, lean waist. He turned to her, gazing down at her, and in his dark, long-lashed eyes Eloise saw desire, felt her own body respond as his mouth swooped to graze her tender lips, parting to his.

It did not take them long to make their way indoors again and take full advantage of the privacy and luxury of the penthouse's master bedroom.

'Welcome to Rome, my sweetest Eloise,' was Vito's soft murmur as he swept her away.

And all thoughts as to why Vito had brought her to yet another hotel instead of his own apartment, even though he was in his home city, fled from her utterly in the heady passion of his lovemaking.

Vito frowned, setting down the phone abruptly and swinging restlessly and with displeasure in the leather chair at his desk in his office. *Accidenti*, this was not what he wanted! Yet his mother had been adamant.

'You absolutely *have* to be there tonight,' she'd said, her tones strained.

But attending the function as his mother was insisting was the last thing he wanted to do—let alone on his first evening back in Rome after so long an absence. What he wanted to do—the way he wanted to spend the evening—was quite different!

To show Eloise Rome by night...

His expression softened. Eloise! Just thinking about her cheered his mood—a mood that had been tightening all day as he'd caught up on corporate affairs here at his head office. He'd wanted the evening off, to spend with Eloise, but now he'd be on show as the head of the Viscari family, no longer only the heir apparent while his uncle and father ran the business between them. Now everything rested only on him—the whole future of Viscari Hotels.

A bleak, painful look showed in Vito's eyes. He leant back in his chair. His father's chair. Four generations had preceded him. And they had created and held on to the legacy that now rested upon his shoulders and his alone.

Except... His eyes darkened now. That legacy was *not* his alone...

Vito's hands gripped the arms of his chair. What had

possessed his uncle Guido to leave his half of the Viscari shares not to his nephew—as had been the long-held understanding in the family, given Guido's lack of children of his own—but to his widow? That disastrous decision had, Vito knew, contributed to his father's heart condition, hastening his premature end fifteen months ago, when he'd been frustrated in his attempts to buy back Guido's shares from his widow Marlene.

Vito knew his parents had always considered her a social-climbing interloper into the Viscari family, hungry for power and influence. And that was why, Vito surmised, Marlene was adamantly refusing to sell her inherited shares, despite the handsome premium offered to her.

His eyes hardened to pinpoints. It was the same reason that lay behind Marlene's most persistent and ludicrous fixation.

When she had married Guido, ten years ago, she had arrived from England with her teenage daughter Carla in tow, and ever since Guido's death one obsession had dominated her. One way for her to cement her position in the Viscari family permanently.

Dream on, thought Vito, his mouth thinning. Marlene could have all the dreams she liked, but she would *never* achieve her ambition—her ludicrous, fantasy-driven ambition.

Vito was adamant. She was *never*, however much she wanted it, going to get him to marry her daughter.

As Vito walked into their suite at the Viscari Roma Eloise's eyes lit up. She got off the sofa and hurried to him to kiss him.

'Miss me?' asked Vito, smiling, throwing himself down on the sofa, loosening his tie and slipping open his top button with relief.

Dio, it was good to see Eloise again, even after the space of only a few hours, and he felt his spirits lift, shifting the pressure that had settled over him after his mother's phone call.

'Beer?' Eloise asked, crossing to the built-in bar.

'Definitely,' Vito said gratefully. 'What would I do without you?' he asked appreciatively, taking a first cold, reviving mouthful.

'Fetch your own beer!' She laughed, nestling into him as he lifted his free arm to draw her against him more closely.

He laughed in return, a carefree sound, stretching out his long legs in front of him. At his side Eloise relaxed into him and his arm around her tightened. The soft expression in her beautiful blue eyes was a balm to his troubled thoughts of the evening's ordeal ahead and what lay beyond.

I have to settle the business of Guido's shareholding. I have to get Marlene to agree to a price and get those shares into my ownership.

Into his head came an image, a memory that haunted him—would always haunt him. A voice imploring him, pleading with him. *'Pay whatever it costs you!'*

Emotion clutched at him like a knife thrust into his side. His eyes shadowed painfully.

He took another mouthful of beer, wanting a distraction from his anguished memories.

'Is everything all right?'

Eloise's soft voice had a note of concern in it, and she was gazing at him questioningly.

I wish I could take her with me tonight!

The function was to be at Guido's opulent villa, to mark the presentation of some of the Viscari artworks to a gallery—an occasion that, as Vito knew only too well, would see Marlene queening it over his mother with relish. His mother would be seething silently, and would make waspish comments about her despised sister-in-law.

Having Eloise at his side would make it more endurable. Vito's eyes glinted sharply. And it would also make it obvious to Marlene that there was no chance he would have the slightest romantic interest in her daughter!

Oh, he and Carla got on well enough—despite the friction between their mothers—and she was highly attractive in her own dramatically brunette way, but she had her own romances and his taste was for blondes. Beautiful, long-legged blondes, with golden hair and blue, blue eyes.

His gaze washed over Eloise's face now. He felt a strange emotion go through him. One he had never felt before and could give no name to. For a moment he wished he had not brought her here to the Viscari Roma, but taken her straight to his own apartment. But would that have been wise? Would it have given her a message he was not yet sure about?

Or am I sure—but not yet admitting it?

That was what caused him to hesitate. And there was another reason, too, for not having taken Eloise directly to his own apartment. His mother would leap to conclusions—conclusions he was not yet ready to draw.

We need time, Eloise and I—time to discover what we truly mean to each other.

Besides, tonight's function would be riven with tensions, and the last thing he wanted was to expose Eloise to the discord twisting through the Viscari family over the matter of Guido's shareholding.

Let me get Guido's shares back first, and then I can focus properly on Eloise—find out what I feel for her and she feels for me.

So for now he only made a rasping noise in his throat

as he answered her question. 'There's a family function I've got to go to tonight that I can't get out of,' he said. 'It's a total pain, but there it is. I'd far rather spend the evening with you. I'd planned on showing off Rome to you.' He made himself smile. 'Trevi Fountain, Spanish Steps...' He gave a sigh. 'Well, it will have to wait till tomorrow night, that's all.'

He swallowed down the rest of his beer and set the empty glass down on the coffee table, absently patting her hand before disengaging himself from her and getting to his feet.

'OK, I'm recharged now. Time to shower and get into the old tuxedo.'

He rubbed his jaw absently. He'd need to shave too. He glanced at the slim gold watch around his wrist as he lowered his hand. Hmm...maybe there was just time for something more enjoyable than a shower and a shave right now...

He held down a hand to Eloise, who was looking up at him, a slightly blank expression on her face. It dawned on him that this was the first time since he'd swept her off to Paris that they wouldn't spend the evening together. His blood quickened. Well, all the more reason for making the most of this brief time before he had to tear himself away and go and do his familial duty—try yet again to sort out the problem of his uncle's shares. But he didn't want to think of that—not right now. Not when he had this precious time with Eloise.

She took his hand and he drew her up to him, using his other hand to spear into the lush tresses of her unbound hair, cradle the nape of her neck and draw her sweet, honeyed lips to his...

She responded immediately, the way she always did when he kissed her. He felt the fire glow within him... within her. He murmured to her in a low, throaty voice as he let her mouth go, only to guide her towards the bedroom...the waiting bed. Desire kindled, quickened... consumed him.

Eloise! The woman he wanted...

It was the last conscious thought he possessed for quite some time thereafter...

CHAPTER THREE

'WELL, I THINK that all went off exceedingly well!' Marlene Viscari's voice was rich with satisfaction as she bestowed a gracious smile upon Vito and his mother, who was standing beside him as she had been all evening, with a fixed expression on her face.

His mother was not the only one with a fixed expression. Carla Charteris, Marlene's daughter, was wearing one too. Vito hadn't seen her for some time, and the last he'd heard of her was that she was in the throes of a torrid romance with Cesare di Mondave, Conte di Mantegna, no less. Presumably, he thought, Carla was as eager to get back to him as *he* was eager to get back to Eloise.

Marlene was speaking again, graciously inviting him and his mother to stay for coffee now that their guests had departed.

'We have so much to discuss,' she said. 'Now that you are back from your little jaunt, Vito!'

Her attempt at lightness and her referring to his essential business tour as a 'jaunt' grated on him—just as everything about her did.

But a moment later his every brain cell went on high alert.

Marlene sailed on. 'And we really do need to settle all this business about the allocation of the shares, do we not?'

Vito tensed, his eyes like gimlets. What was Marlene

up to? He'd been keeping checks on any movement in the markets, listening to the rumour mills around the hotel industry in case Marlene was making any moves to dispose of her shareholding in any way other than by selling to him, but there'd been no sign of any suspicious activity at all.

Not even from Nic Falcone, who had made no secret of being more than keen to take any bites going from Viscari Hotels to feed his ambitious plans for his own start-up hotel chain. Vito had been keeping very close tabs on *that* particular rival!

But surely even Marlene wouldn't be so disloyal to the family she'd married into as to contemplate such a betrayal of her late husband's trust? Nevertheless, he could not afford to ignore her blatant hint just now.

He turned back to his mother. 'Mamma—I'll see you to your car, then stay for coffee with Marlene.'

He exchanged significant eye contact with her and she nodded, casting a sharp look at her sister-in-law, who had a look about her of a cat about to engage with a bowl of cream.

Her expression had changed when he returned to the salon. Marlene was sitting down, Carla standing behind her, and the fixed look on her face was stonier now, so much so that he wondered at it. Was something wrong with Carla?

But it was her mother he must attend to right now. He would hear her out. Too much depended on her. The whole future of Viscari Hotels—the legacy he was dedicated to protecting—rested on his shoulders. Even though the legacy was now fatefully split between himself and Marlene Viscari—who was entirely free to dispose of it however she wanted.

Unless he could find a way to stop her. And he *had* to—somehow he had to!

Into Vito's head sprang the vision he hated to allow in—the vision that sent anguish spearing through him like the point of a blade. His father, stricken after his heart attack, lying in a hospital bed in the last few minutes of his life, his hand clutching at Vito while Vito's mother collapsed, sobbing, at his side.

'You've got to get those shares back—Vito, you must... you must! Whatever it takes—whatever it takes get them back! Pay whatever price she demands. Whatever it costs you! Promise me—promise me!'

And he had promised. What else could he have done with his dying father begging him so? Binding him with an unbreakable obligation.

Unbreakable.

The word sounded in his head now as he heard Marlene out. She was taking her time in getting to the point, asking him about his tour as they drank their coffee, but eventually she set down her cup and glanced briefly at her stony-faced daughter—who had left her coffee untouched, Vito noticed.

'And now,' began Marlene, setting her gaze upon Vito, 'we must look to the future, must we not? The matter of Guido's shares—'

At last! thought Vito impatiently.

A benign smile was settling across Marlene's well-preserved features...a smile that did not reach her eyes. And at her next words he froze.

'My poor Guido entrusted his shares to me, and of course I must honour that trust. Which is why...' her unsmiling eyes held Vito's blandly '... I can think of no better way to resolve the issue than by a means long dear to my heart.'

She paused, and in that pause Vito felt his brain turn to ice.

'What could be better than uniting the two shareholdings by uniting…' she beamed, glancing from Vito to her daughter and back '…the two halves of our family? You two young people together!'

Disbelief paralysed Vito. What kind of farce was Marlene trying to play out? Urgently he threw a look at Carla, waiting for her to express the same rejection and revulsion that he was feeling. But, like a shockwave going through him, he registered that there was no such reaction from her. Instead she was turning a steely, unblinking gaze on him.

'I think,' she said, 'that's an excellent idea.'

He stared, hearing the words fall from her tightly pressed lips.

Oh, hell! thought Vito.

Eloise tossed restlessly in bed. How long could that family function of Vito's go on? It was way past midnight already. She'd spent a forlorn evening. Calling Room Service for a dinner she had only picked at, staring unseeingly at an English-language TV channel. Missing Vito. Feeling left behind.

Finally she had resorted to bed—but the huge king-sized mattress seemed empty without Vito's lean, muscled form.

She tried to think positively. Maybe Vito was spending some time with his mother—after all, he hadn't seen her for weeks now, while he'd been inspecting his hotels. It was natural for her to want to spend a little time with her son.

A thought struck her. *Maybe Vito's telling her about me!*

But what would there be to tell? That elegant Frenchwoman in Nice—one of his exes as he'd admitted—had acidly called her Vito's latest beautiful blonde.

Implying I'm just one in a long line... None of them meaning anything special to him.

But *was* she something special to Vito? And did she want to be?

I want to find out! I want time with him, a proper relationship with him. I want to find out what he means to me and me to him!

Living in Rome, being settled here, would surely show her that? She could get a daytime job as a nanny—maybe to an ex-pat family—while Vito took up the reins of running his family hotel business. She would learn Italian cooking—how to make fresh pasta, even!

She felt her imagination take over, seeing herself cooking dinner for Vito, being part of his everyday life. Eagerness leapt within her. Bringing with it a realisation of just how attractive to her that image was—and why.

It must mean he's important to me—far more than just a passing romance! Mustn't it?

She tossed and turned, knowing for certain only that she wanted Vito back with her tonight. That she missed his company.

She must have fallen asleep eventually, for the next thing she knew she was awake.

'Vito...?' she said, her voice warm with drowsy pleasure.

He was standing by the window of the bedroom, silhouetted against the pale curtains. He didn't move for a moment, but went on looking down at her.

A thread of uneasy disquiet went through her. 'Is everything all right?' she asked.

Vito felt her anxious gaze on him. Savage emotion seared through him. No, everything was *not* all right! It was the damnable, impossible *opposite* of all right!

His fists clenched in his pockets. In his head he heard Carla say, yet again, those fateful words.

'I think it's an excellent idea.'

Fury and disbelief had exploded within him. 'You can't possibly mean that!'

Carla hadn't answered, had only tightened her mouth, while Marlene, with a little light laugh, had got to her feet.

'My dear Vito,' she'd said, relinquishing her daughter's hand, which had promptly closed like a vice over the back of the chair instead, 'you must know how much I would love to welcome you as my son-in-law! It is my long-held dream!'

The triumphant expression in her eyes had made Vito's fury sharpen.

She'd scarcely left the room before he'd rounded on his step-cousin.

'What the *hell* are you playing at, Carla?' He hadn't minced his words. 'You've always stone-walled your mother in her insane obsession about us marrying—just as I have! And as for Guido's shares... I've told you that I'm more than willing to pay a generous price for them—'

Carla's voice had cut in tautly. 'Well, the price is marriage to *me*, Vito.'

He'd shot right back at her, his voice icy. 'Carla, I will not engage in your mother's demeaning and quite frankly distasteful fantasy about the two of us marrying.'

Two spots of colour had flared in his step-cousin's cheeks. 'So you think it *demeaning* and *distasteful* to marry me?'

There had been an edge in her voice that had made Vito pause.

'That isn't what I said,' he'd retorted.

He'd taken a breath—a heavy one—staring hard at her, his eyes narrowing.

'Carla, what's going on here? The last I heard you were

running around with Cesare di Mondave—the two of you were all over each other!'

His eyes had rested on his step-cousin, taken in the sudden paling of her face, the flash of burning emotion in her violet eyes.

Slowly, words had fallen from him as realisation had dawned. 'So that's it—he's finished with you, hasn't he?'

The two spots of colour in her cheeks had flared again. 'You are not the only one, Vito, who considers it "de-meaning and distasteful" to marry me,' she said tightly.

Immediately his expression had changed. 'Oh, Carla, I'm sorry.' His voice had been sympathetic—genuinely so. 'Sorry because…well, to speak frankly, it was always going to end that way. The Conte di Mantegna can trace his bloodline back to the ancient Romans! He's going to marry a woman who can do the same! He might have af-fairs beforehand, but he'll never marry a woman who—'

Carla's voice had sliced across his. 'A woman, Vito, who is about to announce her engagement to another man!'

There had been viciousness in her tone—clear and knifing.

'And marrying me is the only way you're going to get those shares back!'

She'd stormed off, leaving him to feel the pitiless jaws of Marlene's steel trap biting around his guts. Jaws he still felt now as he stood looking down at Eloise.

Eloise! She could blot out for him the trap that had been sprung.

He lowered himself down upon the bed, sweeping her up into his arms. Her soft, slender body was like swans-down in his embrace, her hair like silk, her skin as soft as velvet. He crushed her to him and she murmured to him. Words that were like balm to his stormy soul.

This was where he wanted to be! Here, with Eloise.

He hugged her again, and as he did so he could feel her breasts peaking against the fine lawn of his dress shirt, feel their crests grazing him...arousing him. His mouth nuzzled into the silken hair, seeking the satin skin beneath, and he glided his lips over her throat, her jaw, soon reaching their goal—the soft, parting lips that sought him, too, clinging to him.

He heard her give the soft little moan that he knew so well was a presage of her growing response to him. He gloried in it...revelled in it. He deepened the kiss, his hands going to his shirt buttons to free him from all this unnecessary clothing. Free him from the jaws of the trap that had been sprung on him. Free him to find what he sought most.

Eloise in his arms and he in hers, her body welcoming his, her mouth clinging to his, her breasts swelling against him, her thighs parting for him, taking him into her, taking him to the only place he wanted to be—the place only she could take him.

The rest of the world melted away like honey on a heated spoon—melted and flowed and became only and entirely what he was feeling now, what he was doing now. Because there was nothing else. Nothing else mattered and nothing else existed—only this, only now...

Only Eloise.

And when the fire had consumed him, consumed them both, and after a long, long burning died away, leaving only the warm, sweet glow that was their tangled limbs, their clinging bodies, only then did the words form in his head.

I'm not losing this!

'Is everything all right?'

Eloise's voice was rich with concern. She'd asked Vito that question last night but he hadn't answered, only swept her away to the sensual paradise he always took her to, blotting everything out except the bliss of his possession. Blotting out the unease and disquiet that had nipped at her when he'd come into their bedroom, gazing almost sightlessly down at her with his tense stance, his closed face...shutting her out.

That same unease came again now, as they breakfasted out on the roof terrace of their suite. There was an air of abstraction about Vito, despite his sunny airy smiles and words.

'Everything's fine,' Vito assured her, making his tone as convincing as he could. He would not trouble Eloise with his troubles.

But even as his gaze lingered on her another woman intruded into his vision. Carla, lashing out in the pain of rejection by her lover, who had spurned her in order to marry a woman from his own aristocratic background, driven to make that outrageous ultimatum to save her own stricken pride.

It was the only way to get Guido's shares back.

Frustration seethed in him—and more than frustration. Grief—tearing, abject grief.

Again he recalled his last memory of his father—begging him with his dying breath to get back the shares that would safeguard Viscari Hotels, protect the legacy that was Vito's duty to pass on to his own son, to the next generation.

And the memory of his own grief-stricken voice, making that promise to his father—the last words his father would hear him say before sinking into unconsciousness and death...

How can I betray that promise? Betray what he begged me to do in the last moments of his life?

Emotion knifed him like a blade in his heart. How

could he betray his father? Break the promise he'd made that nightmare day?

'Vito?'

Eloise's voice invaded his consciousness, made him refocus on her. He put a smile on his face, though it was an effort. But for Eloise he would make that effort.

I don't want her affected by any of this—it's too grim, too damn awful!

No, he wanted her protected—insulated. Until he was free of this hideous nightmare closing in on him.

When it's all over—when I've got those shares back—then...

Then he would be free to do what he wanted—focus on Eloise, on discovering just what she meant to him.

Discovering whether she's the one woman for me.

But there was no chance of that yet—not until he'd found a way to smash his way out of the trap that Marlene had sprung on him to fulfil his deathbed promise to his dying father.

'Sorry,' he said, trying to hide the effort it cost him, 'I'm planning my work day already. Speaking of which—I really have to make a move and head to the office.'

He smiled at Eloise apologetically, scrunching up his napkin and getting to his feet, downing his coffee as he did so. Leaving her was the last thing he wanted to do. But he had to get to his desk. Find a way—somehow!— to extricate himself from Marlene's trap.

As she watched him leave Eloise's eyes were troubled.

Is he finishing with me? Is that why he's being like this? Evasive?

The questions were in her head before she could stop them. Bringing with them a painful clench of her stomach. A painful self-knowledge. A painful truth.

I don't want my time with Vito to end.

* * *

Vito sat at his desk—the desk his father had once sat behind. The pressure in his head tightened. He heard Carla's shrill, vicious voice—*'Marrying me is the only way you'll get those shares back!'*

Forcibly, he fought down his anger. Maybe in the morning light his step-cousin would realise how impossible—how insane—her demand was. Maybe Cesare di Mondave would rush back to her and ask her to marry him.

The brief flare of hope died instantly. He didn't know Cesare well, but he knew enough of him to be sure that *il Conte* would have some aristocratic female lined up somewhere in the background as his eventual bride-to-be, once he'd done playing the field with sultry, voluptuous types like Carla Charteris.

A pang of sympathy for her shot through him, despite the ugliness of the scene last night. If Carla really had fallen hard for Cesare di Mondave, however unwise that had been, he could only pity her. Losing someone you'd fallen in love with would hurt badly...

Not that he'd ever been in love himself.

Without conscious thought, he found Eloise's beautiful image in his head. Eloise, who had literally fallen at his feet and whom he had lifted up into his arms—his life. Emotion surged within him. Whatever it was he felt about Eloise, one thing he knew with absolute, total certainty. He did not want to part with her—not yet! No way was his romance with her played out.

But until he had sorted out the unholy mess of Guido's shares he was not free to think of Eloise. He felt his teeth grinding. Here he was, one day back in Rome, and Marlene thought she could corral him with her ludicrously offensive scheming. His expression sharpened. She had made no such move while he'd been making his tour of the European hotels.

So why don't I just take off again? If I'm not in Rome, she and Carla will be stymied.

So where to go? Somewhere far away… The Caribbean would be ideal! The latest addition to the Viscari Hotels portfolio was taking shape on the exclusive island of Ste Cecile—he could combine a site visit with whisking Eloise away from this impossible situation here in Rome!

Mood lifting, Vito reached for the phone, wanting to tell her immediately. It rang as he touched it and he snatched it up impatiently, eager to get rid of whoever was phoning him.

It was his director of finance.

'What is it?' he asked, trying to hide his impatience.

'I've just had a phone call,' came the reply, and Vito could immediately hear the note of clear alarm in his voice. 'A financial journalist I know—asking for a comment on a rumour that's just hitting the wires that Falcone is in discussion with Guido's widow about her shareholding. What do you want me to say?'

Vito froze. The new hotel in the Caribbean, and his trip there with Eloise, went totally out of the window.

Fifteen minutes later, his face stark with anger, he was confronting his step-cousin in her apartment in the Centro Storico.

'Carla, you can't go on with this! It's madness and you know it!'

Marlene was obviously flirting with Falcone to hasten her nephew's consent to marry her daughter. Surely to God Carla could see how insane the idea was? They'd always got on well enough, and he'd kept an eye out for her when she'd arrived in Rome as an awkward teenager while she found her feet socially. And she was not responsible, after all, for her mother's unpopular marriage to his uncle.

'You haven't the slightest interest in marrying me!' he bit out.

'Actually,' she snapped back, her stony gaze flashing into bitter animation, 'I *do*! I want *everyone* to see me marry Vito Viscari!'

'What you want,' Vito ground out, 'is for *Cesare* to see you marry me—that's all!'

'Yes! And then he can go to hell—for ever!' There was all the venom and all the fury of a woman scorned in her voice.

'And after the wedding?' Vito came back with angry sarcasm, determined to make her see reason. 'When Cesare realises what he's lost—then what? You're stuck married to me!'

But her eyes only glittered manically. 'I shall throw parties! Huge parties! And everyone will see how totally, blissfully happy I am!'

He gave a heavy, defeated sigh. For 'everyone' read 'Cesare' again.

He played his last card. Looked her straight in the eye. Expression totally serious. Spelled it out to her.

'Carla, it's impossible for me to marry you. I'm...involved with someone else—someone I met in England.'

There—he had said it. Stated it openly.

The words hung in his head, portentous. But all he got from his step-cousin was a harsh, derisive laugh.

'What? Another of your endless parade of blondes?' she countered. 'Don't trot that line out, Vito! I know you! Women come and go in your life like butterflies—they never mean anything to you!' Her expression altered suddenly, twisting with pain. 'Just as I never meant anything to Cesare—'

She broke off abruptly, her expression venomous again, but this time with a haunted, manic look in her eyes.

'So—like I said—if you don't want my mother to sell Guido's shares to Falcone you'll announce our engagement! Right away, Vito, *right away*!'

Her voice was rising, and he could hear the note of hysteria plain in it. If he went on any more she'd just threw a full-blown fit of hysterics.

For one long, angrily fulminating moment he went on glaring at her, her words knifing in his head. Then, without another word, he strode from her flat, fury burning in him.

His own words echoed in his head—*I'm involved with someone else...*

Eloise! Her beautiful, trusting face lifted to his.

I can't do this to her.

Resolution speared in him. Whatever it took, there had to be a way—there *had* to be—of stalling Marlene, of extricating himself from her daughter's desperate, drowning clutch that was trying to drag him down with her.

As he climbed into his waiting car his mobile rang and he glanced at it angrily. It was his mother, and he knew he had to answer it—knew, too, that he could not let her know what Marlene was doing now, touting Guido's shares to his rival to force his hand.

But at his mother's first panicked words, Vito knew it was too late for prevarication.

'Vito! *That woman* has just phoned me! She's threatened to sell Guido's shares to Falcone if you don't announce your engagement to Carla—so you've got to! You've just *got* to!'

'Mamma,' he said in a hollow voice, 'you cannot mean that...'

There was a stifled cry down the line. 'Vito, you made a *vow* to your father! He begged you with his dying breath!

Don't betray him, Vito—don't betray your own father. You promised to get Guido's shares back, and you can't break that promise—you *can't!*'

He swallowed. 'Mamma, I cannot do what Marlene demands—'

'You must! Vito, you must!' There was desperation in her voice.

He closed his eyes. He could hear how distraught she was. He had to calm her down somehow, anyhow. 'Mamma—listen. *Listen.* I will put out an announcement. OK?'

It wasn't OK—it was total opposite of OK—but it would buy him something that, right now, was the most vital thing for him to get. Time—time to control this runaway situation. It would give him time to manoeuvre, to come up with a way out of this, time to *think!*

He heard the rush of emotion and relief in his mother's voice. 'Oh, thank goodness! I knew you would never, *never* break your promise to your father, my darling son!'

Automatically, his mind racing, Vito went into soothing mode, seeking to calm her—get her off the line so he could focus on how to neutralise Marlene, think through the implications of what he'd just agreed to.

It's an announcement, that's all—it's not a wedding! That's all Carla really wants—to shove her engagement to me into Cesare's aristocratic face in order to save her own face. And I can go along with that—just for now. Until I can find a way to calm her down, get her onside so that the two of us can persuade Marlene to sell Guido's shares directly to me without this farce of me marrying her daughter!

He sat back, his expression steeled. He was playing for time, that was all. He was staying Marlene's hand, placating Carla, calming his distraught mother—finding a way out, a solution. A means to keep his promise to his dying father.

He headed back to his office. His first priority—after authorising that damn announcement—was to scotch those rumours about Falcone getting hold of any of the Viscari shares. He'd need to speak to his direct reports and his board members, to industry analysts, financial journalists... His mind raced down the list.

And, above all, he had to speak to Eloise.

You can't announce your engagement to Carla and not explain the situation to Eloise!

He swore again. The need to get back to his office, do what had to be done there, was overwhelming. Rapidly, his mind raced. He could make the calls from his hotel suite, then talk to Eloise. Explain—

Explain what? Dio mio! *Explain I'm going to get engaged to another woman!*

Another curse of burning frustration dropped from his lips.

I didn't want any of this! All I wanted was to have Eloise with me in Rome—just her and me, being together, exploring our relationship, finding out what we mean to each other. Time together.

And now Marlene and Carla were smashing that to pieces. Caring nothing at all for the complications of his own life right now. Of what was important to *him*.

But, like icy water washing over him, he knew what was really overriding what he wanted. He *had to* fulfil the promise he'd made at his father's deathbed.

A hard, heavy weight pressed down on him. There was no escape. None. This was happening at the very, very worst time. But he must not let it endanger what he had with Eloise.

But how to keep her safe from it? Away from all the gossip that would inevitably break out once his engage-

ment to Carla was announced? He would never expose
Eloise to that!

A surge of protectiveness went through him as a possibility occurred to him—not perfect, but at least doable.

*I'll take her to Amalfi—she can stay there, waiting
for me. I'll explain why—ask for her patience, her trust,
while I extricate myself from Marlene's trap, give Carla
time to see sanity. To come down from the hysterics she's
throwing all over the place!*

But, even though he knew that getting Eloise out of
Rome was essential, a sense of impending loss assailed
him. He didn't want to park Eloise down on the coast—
he didn't want to part with her *at all*, not even for a short
while! Pressure like a vice crushed his skull. Pressure
from his uncle, who had willed away half the Viscari legacy, from Marlene, hell-bent on forcing his hand, from
Carla, intent on hitting back at the man who'd spurned
her, and from his father, who had bound him with an unbreakable chain of love and loyalty, and his mother, desperate for him to accept that chain around him.

For an instant a vision flared in his mind—a vision
so unbearably tempting he almost reached out his hand
to seize it.

*He and Eloise, walking hand in hand along a tropi-
cal beach in the moonlight. The Caribbean waves kissing their bare feet in the warm surf. Far, far away from
here—far, far away from all that assailed him now! Free,
oh, blissfully free of it all!*

Let Marlene do her worst! Let her! Let his uncle's
damn shares pass out of the family.

*I could do it—I could let it happen. I could grab Eloise
by the hand and fly away with her...leave all this behind
me. Just be with her.*

The vision hung in his head like a jewel, and his longing to seize it was painful inside him. Then, as the vice

around his skull tightened, he let the vision go. Dull, piti-less resignation filled him. He couldn't run—he couldn't abandon his duty, his responsibility.

I have to see this out. It's a battle I have to face—and find a way to win.

Because one thing he was adamant about. Whatever price he was going to pay for Guido's shares, it was *never* going to be marrying his uncle's stepdaughter.

CHAPTER FOUR

ELOISE'S EXPRESSION OF delighted surprise at his arrival at their suite in mid-afternoon was a balm to Vito. As he caught her hands, lowering his mouth to her uplifted lips, he felt his spirits lift—as they always did when he saw her.

'This is wonderful!' she was exclaiming, her voice warm. 'I didn't expect you till this evening. I was about to go down to the pool. I've been out exploring this morning—I found the Spanish Steps and the Trevi Fountain!'

Vito smiled, basking in the expression in her face, the open glow in her cerulean eyes. Oh, she might have to stay discreetly out of sight in Amalfi, but only for as short a time as he could manage.

I'll explain what I've got to do, and why, and she will understand. I know she will!

He could trust her—he knew he could. Trust her to understand just what he was up against. He'd wanted to insulate her from all this mess around Guido's shares, but now that he had no choice but to involve her he knew he could rely on her sympathy, her cooperation. On her patience in waiting for him finally to be free to focus only on her.

He drew back, making some comment about her morning's expedition, then shrugged his jacket from him, loosening his tie and turning up his cuffs. Keeping his voice as deliberately casual as he could, he said, 'I've got some phone calls to make, but while I do throw a few things together.' He smiled, his gaze caressing. 'We're going to spend the weekend in Amalfi!'

He waited for the expression of delight he had expected to cross her face, as it had done whenever he'd announced their next destination in Europe, but instead there was a different expression. One of confusion, uncertainty.

'But we've only just got to Rome,' she replied.

'I know,' he said soothingly, 'but... Well...' His mind raced. 'Something's come up, and that's why I want us to get a weekend away.'

That was what he wanted—one last weekend with Eloise before he endured taking on the appearance of a man engaged to Carla Charteris for however long it took him to extricate himself from it.

'Is it...is it just the weekend we'll be away?' Eloise was asking, and Vito had to focus on what she'd said.

'Well, why not pack everything?' he returned, again seeking to make his tone casual. 'In fact,' he went on, as if the thought had just struck him, 'maybe you'd like to stay on there—it's a particularly beautiful stretch of coastline, as I'm sure you know, and the Viscari Amalfi has a spectacular clifftop location. You'll like it far more than here in Rome, I promise you.'

He bestowed a warm, reassuring smile on her. But once again he saw only doubt and uncertainty in her eyes.

He dropped a kiss on her forehead. 'I'll join you down there again as soon as I can get away from here. Things are a bit...pressured right now.'

Had an edge got into his voice? He didn't know—knew only that there was a faint frown on Eloise's brow and her eyes were searching his. Discomfort filled him—he didn't want to have the conversation he would have to have with her right now. He would explain everything to her tonight, when they were safe at the Viscari Amalfi. Right now his overriding priority was to get on the phone and crush the speculation that Nic Falcone might be getting hold of any Viscari shares.

He glanced at his watch. 'Eloise—I have to make those calls. You get packing, OK?'

He smiled distractedly and went off to the small office that the suite came with, immediately putting a call through to his finance director to assure him that, whatever rumour was circulating about Falcone, it was without any foundation. As to his forthcoming engagement—he would say not a word for the moment. Time enough to deal with that when it hit—and when Eloise was safely in Amalfi.

It was complicated, it was stressful, it was damnable—but he *would* pull this off. And then finally—dear God, *finally*—when all the shares were back in Viscari possession, when Marlene had been seen off, and the spirit of his father was at peace, he could focus on Eloise.

And find out just what she meant to him.

But now was not the time to think about Eloise—about why he had no intention of doing without her yet.

The call to his financial director connected, and immediately Vito focused only on that.

For now...just for now... Eloise would have to wait.

Listlessly, Eloise opened the lid of the suitcase she'd extracted from the closet. It was ungrateful of her, she knew, but she really didn't want to go down to Amalfi. For weeks and weeks now her life had been a non-stop parade of packing and unpacking, one hotel after another.

But Vito wanted to be off—yet again.

Another frown furrowed her brow, anxiety pecking at her eyes as she mechanically started to transfer her clothes from where she'd hung them up only a couple of days ago. What had Vito meant when he'd suggested that she might like to stay on in Amalfi after the weekend?

She felt a stab in her side.

Oh, Vito—don't you want to be with me?

Was that it? The stab came again. Was this his way of finishing with her? Of turning her into one more of his legion of *ex-blondes*, like that woman in France.

She felt her expression tighten, a clawing in her stomach. Whatever uncertainties she had as to how much Vito meant to her, the thought of him finishing with her like this was showing her a mirror to her feelings, throwing them into sharp focus.

I don't want him to finish with me!

That was the cry that came now, silently, as she folded and packed her clothes. That was what dominated her mind as emotion welled in her. She did not know if she was in love with Vito—did not know whether she wanted him to be the one and only man in her life, to make her life with him—but she knew by the stab that came again that she did not want him finishing with her...

I don't want us to be over! I don't! I don't!

She closed her suitcase, heart heavy, and as she did so heard the bell at the door to the suite ring. A long, insistent sound. She frowned—then realised it must be for Vito. Maybe he'd sent to the office for some documents to be delivered.

She walked into the reception room, hearing his voice in rapid Italian coming from the office. He sounded... *different*. Though she could not understand what he was saying, there was a terse, insistent tone to his voice, and it was bereft of his usual laid-back, full-on charm.

The doorbell sounded again—longer this time. Eloise pulled open the door.

A woman sailed in. She was around her own age, with dark, striking looks, chicly dressed in a vivid cerise outfit, her face in immaculate full make-up, dramatic violet eyes, and brunette hair coiled in a serpentine mass at the nape of her neck. She looked, Eloise could not help but register, a total knock-out.

For a moment—just a moment—Eloise thought she could detect a kind of stricken look on the woman's face. Then it vanished. Hardened. The dark violet eyes looked past her, through the open door to the bedroom to the suitcase on the bed.

'Good,' said the woman, 'you're packing.'

Eloise blinked. It seemed an odd thing to say, especially as Eloise had no idea who this woman was. But presumably, she reasoned, the woman was something to do with Vito.

'Er...yes,' she made herself reply. 'Vito and I are going to Amalfi.'

In a flash, the woman's expression changed, emotion ripping across it. 'Oh, no, you're not!'

She strode in, pushing right past Eloise.

Dazed and shocked, Eloise could only stare at her, bewilderment on her face. She was bewildered, too, as she registered that the woman had spoken to her in English—English that was completely unaccented.

'Excuse me,' she said faintly, 'but who *are* you?'

The woman rounded on her. strong emotion in her eyes. 'Vito hasn't told you yet, has he?' she said.

That stricken look flashed again in those violet eyes. She took an intake of breath, hissing like a snake. It was audible to Eloise, who was standing there looking even more bewildered.

'Told me what?' Eloise uttered falteringly.

The woman stared at her, her eyes like points of light. 'I'm Vito's fiancée,' she said.

The world seemed to tilt, as if Eloise were hurtling off a plunging platform. Her mouth gaped open. There seemed to be a vacuum in her lungs. No air could get in. No oxygen. She gasped, but still no oxygen went in. She could feel dizziness in her head and then, out of nowhere, nausea biting like a wolf in her stomach.

She stepped back. Staggered. Clutched the wall for support. *'What?'* she gasped. 'You *can't* be!'

Daggers knifed from the brunette's eyes. 'Well, I *am*,' she said.

There was bleakness in her voice, but Eloise was deaf to it. All she could see was the woman looking at her, with that stricken look on her face that must be an echo of her own expression.

The woman sighed harshly, her face convulsing. 'Look,' she said, with a kind of twisted pity in her voice, 'you need to know—Vito's *always* got a blonde draped over him! You're just one more. So don't think you're anyone special! He'd have finished with you anyway soon enough. It's what all men do. *All* of them!'

The woman's voice seemed to break a fraction, and her eyes flashed with pained bitterness.

'So get out while you can—go back to England. Vito's marrying *me*! You wouldn't understand why—and you don't need to! But there's no way you're staying on here. Just be *glad* you're shot of him! I'm doing you a *favour*.'

Her words were cutting into Eloise, into her flesh. Her face looked bleached. This couldn't be true—it just *couldn't*.

Then suddenly into the nightmare footsteps sounded, rapid and hard, coming down the short corridor from where Vito was working.

As he erupted into the lounge, his expression furious, Eloise threw himself into his arms.

'Vito! Oh, Vito! Tell me it isn't true! This woman says she's your fiancée! Tell me it isn't true!'

She felt Vito's arms tighten around her, muscles jerking, and she twisted her head to stare back at the woman standing there, who had dropped such a bombshell into her life. Above her head she heard Vito snarl something in Italian she could not understand. She could feel his muscles steeled, taut beneath her clutching hands.

Then the brunette was answering, still in English. 'Well, I'm here now!' she threw back, and again her face contorted with strong emotion. 'And it looks like it's just as well! Don't even *think* of sloping off to Amalfi!' She rounded on Eloise, her voice rising dangerously. 'I won't have it—do you understand me? I *won't*!'

Now there was a note of impending hysterics in her voice.

Eloise felt Vito's arm slash upwards, cutting across the mounting hysteria. '*Basta!* Carla—*enough*!' There was fury in his voice—and a whole lot more.

Then Eloise was clutching at him. 'Vito—please... please tell me it's not true! Tell me you're not marrying her!'

Her eyes were huge and pleading. Bewildered and distraught.

He could see Carla's face contorting, that twisting flash in her eyes. 'Tell her, Vito!'

'Vito, please!' Eloise's voice was faint with dread.

His jaw clenched. Two opposing forces were pulling him apart. There was Eloise, desperate for his assurance—and every instinct in his body wanted to send Carla packing, her and her mother both. Tell them to go to hell—to do their worst! And then, overlying that, in his head like a death knell, there was his father's desperate dying plea to him...

Get them back, Vito—my son, my only son! Get Guido's shares back. Don't let her sell them—I beg you. I beg you with my last breath...

He looked at Eloise's stricken face, heard her stricken voice. 'Tell me it's not true! Tell me you're not marrying her!'

What could he say? How could he say it to either of them? It was impossible—just impossible!

Time—that was what he needed. If he could just get rid of Carla now—get rid of her so he could talk, explain, make everything right with Eloise! Get her to understand what was happening and why.

And there was only one way to get rid of Carla, hysterical as she was. Because if he didn't...

If I deny the engagement—if I send Carla packing the way I want to do more than anything else in the universe right now—then she'll be straight on to Marlene and Marlene will be on the phone to Falcone...

And Falcone would snap up the shares and divide Viscari Hotels in half at a stroke. Destroy what it had taken four generations of Viscaris over a century to build up.

I'll have betrayed my father, my family—given up the legacy I was left to guard. My mother will be devastated.

He took a razored breath. He *had* to buy time—*had* to get Carla out of here believing she had accomplished the coup she'd so clearly come to achieve. *Had* to pack her off so that he could get back to Eloise and tell her everything she needed to know.

Words formed in his head. Words he had to say—words that would cost him more than he'd ever dreamt he'd have to pay.

He looked at Eloise, his face working.

'Yes,' he said, and his voice seemed to be someone else's, not his—never his...not saying these words to Eloise. 'It's true.'

A cry broke from her. High and unearthly. It was like a blade in his lungs to hear it. She reared away from him, jumping to her feet. He did likewise, reaching for her hands again.

'No! Don't touch me! Don't *touch* me!' She backed away, her eyes wild.

'Eloise—I'm sorry. I'm *so* sorry!'

Guilt lacerated him at what he had just said. Words he'd had to say, could not deny. Even though he *would* deny them—explain them—the moment he could.

Crimson-tipped nails snaked around his wrist like a steel cuff. 'Time to go, Vito,' said Carla, with that desperate, manic look still in her eyes. 'We've got an engagement ring to choose!'

His head swivelled. Eyes that should have burned her on the spot lasered her. But he could do nothing except look across at Eloise.

'I have to talk to you,' he said. His voice was hoarse, urgent. 'I have to explain...explain everything. Do you understand me? It's essential that I talk to you!'

Into his words, his expression, his eyes, he poured all that he wanted her to understand. All that he so desperately wanted Carla *not* to understand!

'I'm so sorry! I'm so desperately sorry it has happened like this! I wanted to speak to you earlier—to tell you—to *explain*.'

'Vito!' Carla's nails dug into his wrist.

He prised them free, stepping towards Eloise. She flinched away. He could not bear it that he could not speak openly, truthfully. Could not bear to see her looking at him the way she was—with horror and revulsion on her face, rejection of him in every stricken line of her body.

Eloise—who was always so welcoming, so ardent, so eager for him...

But now there was only rejection. Shutting him out. Turning away from him.

He seized her hand, would not let her tear it away— not until he'd said what he could, what he must. Even in front of Carla.

'I want you in my life, Eloise! I want you and I'll find a way. I'll find a way somehow!'

But there was no understanding in Eloise's stricken gaze. Only blank horror and stark shock.

A rasp came from Carla. There was vehemence in her voice, her flashing eyes. 'No, you damn well *won't*! You *won't* keep her as your mistress! You won't make a fool of me—no man will *ever* make a fool of me again! And you won't make a fool of *her* either!'

Vito ignored her—his only focus was Eloise.

He could see that Carla's words had hit home. Her face was as white as a sheet. *Dio*, he needed to talk to her—to explain. But he could do nothing now. Nothing except say again, with all the urgency in his being, 'Eloise—wait for me! So I can explain.'

His words were disjointed, staccato. Eloise heard them as if from very far away—across a divide, the chasm that had opened between them as if an earthquake had shaken her world to its foundations.

She wheeled around, her hands going to her face. A terrifying sob mounted in her chest, filling her whole being. A sudden wave of nausea assailed her and she turned, rushing into the bedroom to reach the en suite bathroom.

She stood, shuddering, by the basin. Emotion ravaging her. Shock pummelling her. Words pounding in her head.

What am I going to do? Dear God, what am I going to do?

She stared at herself blindly in the mirror. She couldn't stay here—it was impossible!

With hideous mockery she heard Vito's voice.

'I have to explain—'

Her face contorted. Explain? What was there to explain? That woman had said it all—in a single, devastating word.

She was his *fiancée*—and Vito had not denied it. Had admitted it to her face.

A choke almost smothered her.

And I was asking myself if he was the man who would be my life! The love of my life—my husband!

Hot, stinging tears burned in her eyes. Fool, *fool* that she had been!

The words that had been hurled at her forced themselves into her head.

'Don't think you're anyone special!'

She closed her eyes in misery. That was exactly what she'd been thinking—hoping...

But all I was to him was one more blonde...filling in the time until he got married.

A wave of nausea rose again. No, it was even worse than that. Not just until he married.

'You won't keep her as your mistress!'

A sob broke from her. Misery and humiliation and pain. With another sob, she straightened, made herself open her eyes, made herself look at her stricken, tear-stained reflection.

I can't stay here.

That was for certain. Vito had said he would return to 'explain' everything to her, hoping she would 'understand'. Her face hardened, eyes like stone now. Well, his hopes would be in vain. That woman had been right—his fiancée—Vito wouldn't make a fool of her. Not any longer. Not one moment longer.

Stiffly, she turned away, walked back into the bedroom. At least she was already packed. Another sob threatened to break, but she refused to let it. Refused to let any more emotion break through, break *her.*

Numbly, she picked up her suitcase, fetched her handbag. Then she turned and went out of the bedroom, out of the suite, out of the hotel. Out of Vito's life. The life she could no longer be part of. Could never be part of—whatever she might once so stupidly have thought.

As she climbed into the taxi that the doorman had hailed for her she said only one word to the driver.

'*L'aeroporto.*'

A wolf was tearing at Vito's throat as, yet again, he punched 'send' on his phone while his car was log-jammed in the infamous Roman traffic. Eloise wasn't taking his calls, wasn't acknowledging his texts. He'd been inundating her with both non-stop since he'd finally despatched Carla back to her harpy of a mother with a massive diamond on her finger, its glitter echoing the manic glitter still in Carla's eyes.

He was beyond caring—Carla could flaunt the diamond all she wanted. Flaunt it in front of the man who was refusing to marry her, flaunt it in defiance and bitter fury, until she finally came back to earth and accepted the absurdity of what she was doing, the outrageous way she was behaving, and refused to be a pawn for her mother's ambitions.

But all Vito wanted—wanted with all his being—was to get back to Eloise. To explain the trap that he was caught in, and how desperately he needed *time* to force it open and free himself so that he could focus on the one thing in his life he wanted to focus on. Eloise.

On being with her, living with her, having her at his side. Here, in Rome, making a journey together to discover what they meant to each other.

I've got to make it right with her! I can't endanger what we have! She's too important to me!

Even as the words formed in his mind he realised the truth of them. He had realised it from the moment he'd seen Eloise recoil from him and he still felt the stab in his guts that recoil had inflicted.

When I explain everything to her she will understand—I know she will! She always understands...

But he had to get to her first. Had to make sure she was there, waiting for him. Urgently he texted yet again, telling her he was on his way back, that he would be there as soon as he could, telling to wait for him.

But as he drew up at the hotel the doorman stepped forward. And what he told him stopped Vito dead.

The transatlantic flight went on and on. The steady drone of the engines in Eloise's ears was endless. As endless as the bleak bitterness filling her. Over and over again, like a ghastly video loop, the nightmare scene with Vito's fiancée played on in her head, forcing her to see the ugly truth about the man she'd so recklessly, blindly taken on trust. The man who'd swept her off in a whirlwind romantic haze, a wish-fulfilment dream, with a heady intoxication of the senses that had blinded her to his true nature.

All that passion, all that romance, all that devotion—and it had been nothing, nothing at all!

Because all along Vito had known perfectly well that back in Rome was the woman he was going to make his future with, the woman he was going to marry.

No wonder he didn't take me to his apartment! No wonder he didn't take me to that family function that first evening—his fiancée would have been there as well!

He hadn't even intended for her to stay in Rome at all, had he?

I was just going to be stashed away in some little love-nest in Amalfi, to be visited for sordid, secret sex sessions, kept as his convenient mistress.

She felt the nausea rise again from the pit of her stomach, revulsion filling her. And, more than that, pain, a sense of the deepest betrayal. Misery swept over her and she closed her eyes, feeling hot tears seeping beneath her lashes. It hurt—oh, how it hurt!

Memories, a thousand of them, pushed aside that tor-menting video loop, crowded it out. Memories right from that very first moment when she'd gazed up from her sprawl on the airport concourse to see Vito looking down at her. She'd been captivated from the start, from that very first glance of his dark, melting eyes.

Memory after memory bombarded her—the sense of heady excitement and wonder, the tremor of desire building up in her, that incredible, unforgettable first night together, when he had taken her with him to a place so wonderful, so beautiful, that she had never known her body could take her there. And, thereafter, day after day, night after night. Vito...always Vito.

Always Vito.

She choked back a sob. All gone—gone, gone, *gone*! Ripped from her by a truth so ugly that she could not bear it.

Yet bear it she must. There was no other option. No other option but to flee, as she was doing, broken and tearful, yet steeling herself with a bitter anger at how he had lied to her—oh, not in words, but in deeds.

He had no right—no right to romance me! No right to have an affair with me! No right to let me think...

Another sob choked in her throat. No right to let her think...hope...that theirs was a passion that might lead to emotions that would bind them together for all their lives...

When all along he had been planning a very different future for himself.

And there it was, back again in her head, that hideous video loop—his fiancée bursting in, denouncing him, throwing savage pity at her, ripping her stupid, stupid illusions from her. Trampling on everything she had been starting to hope.

Trampling on the dreams she had started to long to come true.

Her hands clenched in her lap and she closed her eyes tighter shut.

And still the flight went on, and on.

When—after a lifetime, it seemed to her—the plane finally landed at JFK, she knew there was only one resolution to keep. She had said it all in that single text she had sent to him, after deleting unread the storm of texts that had arrived on her phone, deleting unheard all the voicemails. One single response from her had said all that needed to be said.

You are the most despicable man I know. Stay away from me for ever. Eloise.

CHAPTER FIVE

I<small>T WAS STILL</small> afternoon in New York, despite the hours since she'd fled Rome. But her mind was in some strange, dislocated no-man's-land which let her stare out of the taxi's window at the busy concrete canyons passing her by on her way through Manhattan.

She'd texted ahead from the airport and received a directive to go straight to her mother's apartment. As she whooshed up in the elevator, having collected a key from the concierge, a little ripple of nausea hit again, but she banked it down. A wave of weariness followed—weariness that went much deeper than the physical, was much more than jet lag. She needed to sleep—to claim oblivion from the devastation in her head.

Inside the apartment, she found the spare room she'd used before, and dumped her case. Her eyes felt as if they were being pressed with weights—she could barely take off her shoes before collapsing down on the bed, pulling back the covers to slide beneath the quilt.

Moments later she was asleep.

She must have slept for hours, adjusting overnight to New York time, for it was morning again when she surfaced. She opened her eyes, blinking. A cup of coffee was being placed on the bedside table beside her.

She shuffled up to a sitting position, pushing her long hair out of her eyes, looking at the person who had put it there, who was standing looking down at her with a questioning look on her face.

She took a breath. 'Hello, Mum,' said Eloise.

'Let me get this straight.'

Eloise's mother's voice was clear, and it penetrated right into her head like a drill.

'You let some spoiled, self-indulgent Italian playboy pick you up—literally!—and you went off with him without a thought, without the slightest hesitation or consideration, got tumbled into bed by him within twenty-four hours, and *then* you trotted along at his heels like a little poodle, only to discover—' her expression was scathing '—that, lo and behold, he not only turns out to have a fiancée waiting for him in Rome, but fully intends to keep you as his handy mistress on the side! Eloise, how *could* you waste yourself on a man like that?'

Eloise closed her eyes. 'I don't know...' she whispered. But she did know—knew exactly how it had happened. *Why* it had happened. 'He seemed so wonderful,' she said brokenly.

Her mother snorted. 'Yes, well, women make fools of themselves every day.' She took a breath. 'I should know. I made an idiot of myself over your father.' She gave a heavy sigh and got to her feet. 'Well, you can stay here as long as you want—though don't waste your time moping over the man! You're well rid of him!' Her voice changed, becoming businesslike. 'Best to start working again. I'll ask around my acquaintances for anyone who might need a nanny—that will take your mind off him.'

Eloise's face paled, and a look of anguish came into her eyes.

Her mother's expression changed again. 'You'll get over it, Eloise,' she said bluntly, but there was a resigned thread of sympathy there as well. Her voice softened a fraction. 'And you got out just in time—unlike me, with you already born and your father deserting us for his brood mare! With *you*, however, it's completely different. No repercussions—thank heavens!'

She glanced at her watch.

'I must go,' she said, back to her habitual brisk tones. 'I'm late for work.'

She brushed her cheek briefly against her daughter's, then walked out, leaving Eloise lying back against the pillows, her face bleak as an Arctic waste.

No repercussions, her mother had said. But she was wrong. Totally wrong.

There was a dark, bleak look in Vito's eyes. It had been there for days—ever since he'd opened that curt, damming text from Eloise. The words were incised into his brain as if with a chisel.

You are the most despicable man I know. Stay away from me for ever. Eloise.

For days, he had rejected her order, continuing to bombard her with texts and voicemails with an increasing sense of desperation…longing for her. He had to find her, talk to her, explain—

But he hadn't found her. She had headed to the airport and vanished. Presumably she had gone back to England—but with dismay he realised he had absolutely no idea where she might be. She'd worked as a live-in nanny—she didn't have an address of her own. She could be anywhere…

He'd set investigators on to it, but they'd drawn a blank. All further texts and calls to her mobile had been blocked.

She does not want me to find her. Wants nothing more to do with me.

And with every passing day, and still no way of finding her, that was what he *had* to accept.

Eloise was gone.

Her absence from his life was a vast, desolate hollow opening inside him—a sense of loss that gave him a bitter answer to the question he had asked about her ever since she'd come into his life.

I wanted to know if she was truly special to me—if she was coming to mean more to me than any other woman I've known.

His mouth twisted painfully. Well, now he knew. She had become far, far more than just one of the women in his life. He knew now that she'd been quite, quite different. Knew by his constant longing for her, his need to see her there, in front of him, holding out her arms to him, lying beside him in his embrace, being with him, at his side, all the time...

To know the answer to that question now, with her absence so unbearable to him, was a cruel irony indeed. As cruel as the pain of missing her so much. As cruel as the frustration that bit into him.

I begged her to wait and hear me out—to let me explain why I said what I did in front of Carla! If she had only given me a chance to explain about Marlene and the shares. Explain about Carla and her manic need suddenly to have a fiancé!

But she had not—she had vanished instead. Rejected him totally.

I thought she would be sympathetic, understanding— like she always was! Always there for me.

But only the malign shadow of Carla was there now, her manic bitterness unabating. He could see it in the blindness of her eyes, the gauntness of her face. He did not care.

And as with each passing day he became bleakly resigned to the fact that he could not find Eloise, he felt a kind of slow fatalism numb him. If Eloise was gone— if she could not be found—then what reason was there to balk any longer at this grotesque way of fulfilling his deathbed promise to his father? Saving Viscari Hotels from dismemberment. Protecting the legacy he had been born to guard.

So, with grim decision, he determined to let Carla have her garish wedding, announcing to the world she had not been rejected by her aristocratic lover but that she was making a dynastic match of her own to fulfil her mother's obsession. But, he spelt it out freezingly to his gaunt-faced step-cousin, within six months the marriage must be annulled. Carla could give any face-saving reason she wanted—he would not care. He would keep Guido's shares, handing over their market value to Carla when they parted.

And then it would be done. Over.

The dreary, crushing numbness pressed down on him. The numbness that would never lift now.

'Time to tidy up your toys, Johnny.'

Eloise's voice was bright. As bright as it was brittle.

Her four-year-old charge was a happy lad, and unspoilt despite his parents' wealth. It was Eloise's task to keep him that way. She had been glad—grateful—to find a post so quickly, via her mother's contacts, and had moved out to the Carldons' massive mansion on Long Island.

Johnny's father was based on Wall Street, at the family banking house, where his mother Laura worked as well, though she planned to work part-time from home once she had her second child. Until then young Johnny needed a live-in nanny. His parents usually stayed mid-week at their Manhattan apartment, putting in the punishing hours that top jobs on Wall Street demanded, so they could spend long weekends on Long Island with their son, so Eloise was often in sole charge of Johnny, alone in the Long Island mansion apart from the Carldons' house-keeper Maria and chauffeur Giuseppe.

It had been an uncomfortable jolt to hear the married couple speak Italian to each other, but Eloise had gritted her teeth and endured it.

Just as she was enduring her entire existence.

There was a bleakness inside her...a tearing misery she could not shed. Her mother's bracing admonition *'You're well rid of him!'* seemed only to make the world bleaker still. She knew the truth of her mother's words—but all they did was pain her more. As painful as the tor-menting memories of how happy she had thought she'd been with Vito, of the shining hopes she'd been filled with.

She could tell herself all she liked that she'd tried to be cautious about her whirlwind romance, that she'd warned herself that it might be nothing more than a starry-eyed infatuation, an intoxicating dream.

Her expression bleached. It hadn't been that at all, though, had it? Not a dream—nothing but a sordid, clan-destine fling with a man promised to another woman.

I wanted to know what I felt about him! Wanted to know if he was going to be the man I'd spend the rest of my life with! I found out the truth too late...

That was the cruelty of it. Her hopes and dreams had already started to weave around him—and now, four thousand miles away from him, they still had the power to haunt her.

A toxic mix of anger and misery filled her, rising up with a familiar sick feeling in her stomach. She fought it back. Oh, what use was there in feeling like this? Her mother was right! She *had* to get over it—*had* to put Vito in the past. Stop her useless anguish over it all! There was no choice for her but to get over him—turn off, smother, kill whatever it was she'd felt for him. No matter what those feelings had been—or might have become—it didn't matter now.

Now, and for her entire future, only one thing was important. There was only one joy to look forward to, only one meaning for her life. Only one way to heal her bruised and battered heart. Only one outlet for the love inside her.

She lifted her chin, fighting the dumb misery inside her. She would *not* let it win. She must not. Her future was changing—changing for ever—and that was *all* she must focus on now!

Emotion welled up in her, fierce and protective. Her time with Vito had been a disaster—but out of it had come a blessing she had not looked for and which now would be the reason for her life.

The only reason.

Another wave of nausea hit her...

Vito stood, stiff and immobile, at the altar rail of the church of Santa Maria della Fiore. Its showy, baroque splendour fitted the tastes of his bride, who was burning with desperation to show the world she was *not* a discarded, spurned creature, too lowly to be *contessa* of an ancient name, but was instead the enviable bride of one of Rome's most eligible and desirable bachelors, her glittering wedding as lavish as Marlene could devise.

All Vito was required to do was go through with it.

Keep his promise to his dying father. Get back his uncle's shares. Make the Viscari legacy safe at last.

Whatever it cost him to do so.

Into his head fleetingly, like a bird soaring high and out of reach, memory flashed.

Eloise—her arms opening to him, drawing him close to her, the scent of her, the fragrance of her hair, the silk

*of her skin, the warmth in her eyes, the tender curve of
her mouth—*

He shook the memory from him. She was gone from
his life. What she had been to him was over. What she
might have become he would never know.

He shifted his stance. What use to think of Eloise now,
as he stood on the brink of marrying another woman? A
woman he did not want, did not desire. But who brought
with her the means to safeguard what his family had built
up for over a century.

All around him he heard the organ music swelling,
the choir's voices lifting, and knew that his bride was ap-
proaching. He heard the congregation rising to its feet,
saw the officiating priest start to step forward. In minutes
now he would commit himself to marriage.

Words thrust themselves into his head as he stood
there, rigid and immobile, as if chained where he stood
by forces he could not defy. Making himself endure it
with a strength he had to find.

*Is this what you want me to do, Papa? Is this how you
want me to get back your brother's shares? Is this the
price you want me to pay for them?*

The choir's soaring voices reached a crescendo before stilling.

Every muscle in Vito's body tensed, as if he were forcing himself to stand stock-still. Carla was beside him, the
folds of her couture wedding dress brushing his leg, her
lace-veiled figure as rigid as his, the rich fragrance of her
heavy perfume cloying.

He did not look at her. Could not. Could only sense
the tension racking her as she stood beside him. Driven
by her own demons.

And she was taking him with her, and for that he
damned her utterly.

The sonorous voice of the priest sounded over his head.

Latin words were murmured and intoned as the words of the wedding service proceeded. Words that would bind them in holy matrimony.

A cold, icy shudder went through him. Clearing the numbing blankness in his mind. The priest was talking again, saying the most potent words of all. Would he take this woman for his wife?

Vito's eyes were on the priest, then on the altar beyond. Then he turned his head slightly, to look at Carla's veiled figure, trembling with tension. He *had* to do this. He had come this far, had done all this, to fulfil his promise to his father. What choice did he have now?

What choice? The question seared in his head. Demanding he answer.

For one long, endless moment he stood silent as that question burned in his head. Then he took a breath and gave his answer...

Everything seemed to have gone into slow motion. Or perhaps it was just his brain that was going slow. He watched the priest incline his head towards him, as if he had not quite caught his response. Behind him, he heard a kind of susurration, like the buzzing of insects. And beside him he could hear Carla give an intake of breath that was like a razor in its sharpness.

And its disbelief.

He turned his head to look at her. She was staring at him. Staring at him through her veil with an expression in her eyes that was something like an alien out of a sci-fi film.

He closed his eyes a moment, then opened them again. 'I won't do this, Carla,' he said.

His voice was quiet, audible only to her. But there was a certainty in it that infused every word.

'I won't do it to me—and I won't do it to you. This is a travesty. An abhorrence. This is not what marriage is about—on any terms, or for any reason. You deserve better. And so do I.'

And so does Eloise—she didn't deserve what I did to her.

A low, scarcely audible sound came from Carla's throat. Her eyes distended and she swayed, her body starting to fold. Instantly Vito's arm came around her. The priest stepped forward to help support her between them, and then Carla's mother rushed forward, consternation on her face as they escorted Carla to the vestry. His own mother hastened after them, anxiety all over her face.

As he helped the stricken Carla to a chair, he turned towards Marlene. His voice, when he spoke, was very calm—but with unbending steel in it.

'I will not go through with this, Marlene,' he said, his eyes boring into hers as fury leapt in her face. 'You may tell everyone that Carla couldn't face marrying me, or that she is ill—whatever you want to say to protect her. But I will no longer be party to your machinations. I will pay you twice what Guido's shares are worth—but I will no longer be blackmailed by you. Do your worst, if you must.'

Behind him came a cry of anguish. It was his mother, rushing forward to clutch his arm. He turned to her, leading her a little way away to give them privacy. This was nothing to do with Marlene or her daughter. This was between his mother and himself.

And his father.

He felt the strength of his resolve to hold dear every value he possessed. Every value that made life worthwhile—that had to guide every life in order for it to be... *honourable.*

'Mamma,' he said now, and his voice was as gentle as his hold on her, though the resolve, the strength, was still in his expression. 'When you stood beside my father at your wedding you promised to love and honour him. And I, too, honour him—which is why I will not bind myself to the promise I made him. To marry Carla would be... dishonourable. Whatever the reasons for such a marriage, they cannot be justified. Neither for her, nor for me.'

He took an unsteady breath.

'I'm sorry that I have not had the courage or the resolution to say this until this moment. I have tried to do my best by my heritage, by my promise to Papa. But not at this price.'

He looked at her stricken face, into her anguished eyes.

'To marry Carla like this would be to dishonour all that I hold dear—all that you and Papa taught me to value. Self-respect, honesty, integrity... I will not strike this devil's bargain—' he cast a punitive look towards Marlene, huddled with Carla '—because it would shame me, it would shame my father, and it would shame you.'

Gently he put his arm around his weeping mother's shoulder. 'Time to go home, Mamma,' he said. 'There is something I must do. Someone I must find.'

Find Eloise.

And find out what she means to me once and for all.

CHAPTER SIX

'WHAT DO YOU say to Nanny Ellie?' Johnny's mother prompted.

'Thank you!' exclaimed the little boy, gazing at the cover of the jigsaw box, which depicted an unfeasibly cute dinosaur.

Eloise had bought it in Manhattan, having taken a day's leave to travel in.

As Johnny lifted off the lid and emptied the wooden pieces on to the table Laura turned to Eloise.

'Well, how did it go?' she asked.

There was both friendliness and concern in her voice.

'Fine,' said Eloise. 'No problems. It's all "steady as she goes".'

'That's great!' Laura said warmly. 'When's your next appointment?'

'Next month—unless something crops up.'

'Let's hope not,' said Laura. 'Keep up the plain sailing!' She smiled. 'Now, why don't you go and put your feet up? Take the evening off. Johnny and I can get stuck into this jigsaw, and John's promised to be home by bathtime.'

'Yay!' contributed her son enthusiastically. 'I like bathtime with Dad. He lets me splash!'

'Does he, now?' said his mother severely, and exchanged a woman-to-woman look with Eloise. Then she turned back to her son. 'OK, so first we need to find the edge bits—especially the corners. Have you got any of those?'

Eloise left them to it, slipping away to her own generous quarters. There was an ache in her that had nothing to do with the day's journey in and out of Manhattan. Johnny was a happy child, and his parents were warm and loving, united in their love for each other and both devoted to their son.

The kind of family Eloise longed to make for herself. The kind of family she'd once thought she might make with Vito—

No! Don't go there! Don't think about those naïve hopes that you once wove into the baseless fabric of your stupid dreams.

She had told myself that maybe their romance was like champagne—warned herself that one morning she might wake to find it flat and stale.

But it hadn't turned flat and stale—it had turned to bitter, bitter gall.

A gall she must swallow. Drink down all her life.

At least she had her mother's support. And there was an irony about that that Eloise found only added to that bitter taste.

'It won't be easy, Eloise, but who said being a woman was ever easy? Certainly not when some selfish male has messed up your life!'

No, it wouldn't be easy. But it had to be done. Her love would have one focus now—one focus alone.

As she closed the nursery door behind her a peal of laughter broke out from Johnny, echoed by his mother. That ache smote her again.

A happy little boy, with a happy, loving family surrounding him, a doting mother and father in a happy marriage together...

That can never be for me. Not now.

Sadness pierced her, haunting the blue of her eyes. She had dreamt all her life of making a happy family...not like her own...and yet now that was beyond her for ever.

Vito threw himself into the chair behind his desk and deep desolation filled him. The board meeting he'd just emerged from had been bruising—slamming into him just what he had done.

What Marlene had done.

She had fulfilled her threat—sold Guido's shares to Nic Falcone. Sold them the very day Vito had walked out of the church. And just now Nic Falcone had sat arrogantly across the boardroom table from him, demanding his pick of the Viscari portfolio—as befitted the new half-owner of Viscari Hotels.

The resulting discussion had been...*difficult*. Grim-faced, along with the rest of his board, Vito had played hardball as much as his position allowed, and finally a memorandum of agreement had been achieved. But the loss of every property that Falcone had taken from him drove a dagger into Vito's heart.

He sat now, a bleak, brooding expression on his face.

Only one prospect could lessen that grievous loss.

Finding Eloise.

I will not give up on her! I cannot!

He had to find her, to discover whether he could salvage anything from the hideous mess he'd made of things, something that was worth fighting for.

The long, grim months without her had only shown him what he had lost when she'd left him. So he'd renewed his efforts to discover where she'd gone, reactivating all his lines of enquiry. But all had drawn a blank. Only one—a wild, maverick attempt—remained. Would it work? *Could* it work? To this point it had not.

His sense of desolation deepened. His expression sombre.

The sound of his phone ringing hardly made him stir. Until the caller started to leave a message. Then, as if an electric current had suddenly galvanised him, Vito snatched up the phone. Heard out the caller.

When the call ended, he promptly summoned his PA. 'I need you to book a flight for me tonight,' he told her.

And then, and only then, did his eyes light with animation. With relief. With an emotion that had not been there for long, deadened weeks.

With hope.

'Wowee! Wowee! Come and *see*!'

Johnny's exuberant call drew Eloise to the nursery window, where her charge was gazing out onto the carriage sweep. The long, low scarlet automobile drawing up with a throaty growl of its powerful engine made her start.

Vito had driven a car just like that…

Instantly memory bit. Her and Vito, cruising along the *autostrada*, her eyes on him. He'd looked so impossibly glamorous and gorgeous, with his designer dark glasses, his hands curved around the wheel, revelling in the power of the steering…

She forced the memory from her head. Vito was an ocean away from her and she had to get on with her life without him—make the future that awaited her now without him. What was the point of thinking about their time together?

She stared bleakly down as the car door opened. As the driver got out.

Faintness drummed at her, and a disbelieving gasp was wrenched from her throat.

It was Vito.

Vito here—now—outside the house. Walking up to

the house, disappearing from view under the porch she could not see from the angle of the nursery window. She felt numb with shock.

Johnny raced to the nursery door. 'I want to go down and see the car!' he exclaimed.

The next moment the house phone was ringing, and Johnny dashed to snatch it up.

He turned excitedly to Eloise. 'The car man wants to see *you*! Come on, come on, come on!' He tugged her towards the door.

His little hand made no impact on her total immobility. Her total inability to think, to pull one shred of rational usage from her brain.

Only one phrase existed in it.

It's Vito—it's Vito—it's Vito...

But it couldn't be. It was impossible. Completely impossible. Vito was in Italy. In Rome. With his wife. It could not be him because he did not know where she was. So how had found her? And why—?

Raggedly, her mind zig-zagged incoherently, her thoughts flying everywhere, borne on emotions that were tumbling about crazily inside her, like rocks in a washing machine. Urgently she sought to get a grip on herself, to fight through the shock smashing through her.

Johnny let go of her, yanking open the door, haring out. With a start, she hurried after him—he was her charge and she must look after him. But at the top of the stairs she froze.

Vito was in the hall below, talking to Giuseppe. She heard Italian, saw Giuseppe shake Vito's hand. Saw Vito turn his head as Johnny tugged urgently on her hand to go downstairs. Saw the expression on Vito's face.

'Eloise!'

He had taken off his dark glasses and he was just staring at her. Staring at her and drinking her in with his eyes as if she were water in a parched, parched land.

'Eloise...' He said her name again. A faint, exhalation of breath, like the sighing of the wind.

She met his gaze. Felt herself reel with the force of it.

Then, from the door at the back of the hall, the rotund figure of Maria erupted, rushing up to Vito, breaking into voluble Italian. Vito was smiling at her, and Eloise could hear him replying, his voice warm. Thanking her.

Numb still, Eloise let Johnny tug her downstairs. He broke free of her at the bottom and rushed to Vito, pulling at his trouser leg.

'I *need* to see your car!' he exclaimed.

Vito looked down at him, hunkered down beside him. Smiled at the little boy. Against her will, Eloise felt her heart skip a beat.

He used to smile at me like that.

No—she mustn't think of that...mustn't remember.

'Do you, now?' Vito was saying, obviously amused by his eagerness.

'Yes!' confirmed Johnny, oblivious, as only a four-year-old could be, to the tension, the atmosphere blazing all around him. 'Come on, come on!'

He seized Vito's hand with all the confidence of a well-loved child and made to drag him to the front door.

Vito straightened, gently disengaging his hand from Johnny's. 'In a while, OK?'

He ruffled Johnny's hair, in a friendly, easy fashion, and again Eloise felt emotion scissor through her. But not memory this time.

No! Don't think of that either—just don't! Don't!

She'd never seen Vito with children before—never seen this easy, unforced attitude. His obvious amusement. Enjoyment. As if it came supremely naturally to him.

The scissoring emotion came again.

Then Giuseppe was stepping forward. 'Why don't I show you?' he said to Johnny, glancing at Vito for agreement.

Vito nodded, a grateful look on his face. Giuseppe swept Johnny away, and Maria bustled forward busily to open the door to the library, beckoning to Vito...and then to Eloise.

But Eloise could not move. Vito's eyes went to her, rooting her to the spot. The easy smile that had been there for Johnny had gone. Now his expression was as grave and as stark as the tension visible in every line of his body as he walked towards her at the foot of the stairs.

'Eloise—I have to talk to you.'

His voice was low and vibrant. With the same urgency in it that she had heard the day he'd told her that he was indeed marrying the woman who had stormed into their suite, stormed into her life, destroying everything in her path. Trampling over what they had...what they might have had.

Hideously aware of Maria, still holding the library door open, Eloise stumbled past her into the spacious room. Vito strode after her. Only when Maria had shut the door, giving them privacy, could she speak.

'How did you find me? It's impossible that you have!' Her voice came out high-pitched, half strangulated.

'Yes,' Vito said, his voice stark, like stone scraped bare, 'you *made* it impossible. And I know why, Eloise— I understand why you did.'

Her eyes flashed. However Vito had found her—and for whatever reason!—it was impossible for her to have anything more to do with him. She felt emotion sear in her. But it didn't matter how her eyes were drinking him in, how faintness was drumming inside her just at the very sight of him, because everything was still impossible—totally impossible!

He was speaking again, and she made herself hear as he reached inside his jacket pocket, took out a much-folded piece of paper, colourful and glossy. He opened it out, and it looked to Eloise as if it had been torn from a magazine.

'This is how. Maria saw it and got in touch with me.'

He held the page out to her. She wouldn't approach. Her head went up. Emotions pounded inside her, but there was only one that she could allow. Anger. Only anger.

'However you did it, you've wasted your time! If you're here to tell me you'd like me to come back with you and be your adulterous little bit on the side, your convenient mistress, your *poodle*, you can forget it! Go back to your wife, Vito! Go back to her. Because I didn't want to know then, and I don't want to know now—I'll *never* want to know!'

She could see a tic working in his cheek. 'Please look at this, Eloise.' He pushed the piece of paper towards her, across the table, rotating it so that it was facing her.

She could see the photo on it even from this distance. It was Vito—and her.

She was in evening dress, and Vito was standing beside her—it must have been at one of the endless round of cocktail parties during his hotel tour, when she'd followed him around like a trusting little poodle...

But there was another photo, too, on the facing page—just of Vito by himself. It was his head and torso, face-on, looking at her directly off the page.

And beneath it was a headline that blazed in huge letters—words in Italian. She knew the type of magazine it was—one of those ritzy, glossy weeklies that focused on celebrities and high society.

'It says,' Vito intoned, and there was something strange about his voice, '*"Help me find her, my most beautiful Eloise!"* I had to find you, Eloise. I *had* to. Because I have something to tell you—and something to beg of you.'

He walked towards her, his stride purposeful. His eyes were on her, never moving, not for a second, fixed on hers like a laser beam as he came up to her. There was only a metre between them. His closeness was unbearable. He was out of reach. Barred from her by marriage... by betrayal.

'I don't want to know! I don't know want to hear!' she cried, shaking her head as if to block out his voice. Trying to defend herself by going on the attack.

Emotions warred within her—the blaze of overwhelming reaction at seeing him again burning through her like a forest fire. Doused by the cold, fierce fury at what he had done to her.

She forced words through her narrowed throat. 'I won't go back to you, Vito! I told you that you were despicable—'

'Yes,' he said tightly, 'I behaved despicably to you. But...' He took a scissoring breath. 'I didn't intend to. I was...trapped.'

A bitter laugh broke from Eloise. 'Yes, that's what married men always say! Oh, don't tell me, Vito—your wife doesn't understand you, does she?'

There was vicious mockery in her voice. Fuelling her anger. Anger she had to keep fuelled, filled to the brim, spilling over into the hostile venom she was hurling at him.

Because if she didn't feel anger at Vito, then...

No, I can't allow myself to feel anything else! I can't... I can't!

His face had tightened even more. His cheekbones were exposed like carved marble, his mouth like a whip. She could see the steeled tension in the set of his shoulders, how he was holding his body rigid.

'I have no wife.' The words fell like stones from him. 'The wedding never went ahead.'

The expression in his eyes made her breath stop. There was a starkness in them that was like bleached bone.

'That's why I am here, Eloise. To tell you that.'

Her face convulsed. For a moment—just a moment—emotion flared in her like phosphorus. A longing so intense it burned within her. She felt her hand flutter to her abdomen, felt the longing burn again. Longing to clutch at the dream that hovered, soaring now at what he'd just told her.

No wife—he has no wife! So could we—oh, could we...?

But then the flare was extinguished. What difference did it make? What difference could it make? After what he'd done to her.

'And do you expect me to throw myself into your arms?' she cried. 'Tell you I forgive you for what you did to me? Is that what you expect?'

Vito's mouth tightened. He shook his head. 'I expect nothing, Eloise.' He drew a heavy, leaden breath audibly into his lungs. 'I have come here only to explain to you why I did what I did.'

He paused, not letting his eyes drop from hers.

'I ask only that you listen to me now.' He swallowed. 'I know you refused to let me talk to you, refused to let me try and explain, and I can understand why—but now that...that I have no wife after all, I beg only one favour from you. To hear me out.'

His stark gaze bored into her again.

'Will you grant me that favour?' he asked.

Eloise felt her mouth tighten, her chin lift. She felt as heavy as lead.

'You intend to trot out excuses for why you behaved the way you did? Is that it?' There was a coldness in her voice she did not bother to hide.

He gave an infinitesimal shake of his head. 'Not excuses—reasons. Reasons I had no chance to explain to you in Rome. Reasons I must give you now.'

He took a breath, hoping she would let him explain before she fled from him.

'I agreed to marry my step-cousin, Carla,' Vito said, as if cutting the words from himself, 'because it would allow me to obtain the shares in Viscari Hotels that her mother, Marlene, had inherited from my uncle Guido— her late husband. That was the reason. The *only* reason.'

Eloise reeled back, her face paling as if he had struck her, as his words impacted on her. She stared at him, gall rising in her. 'You traded me for a handful of shares,' she said.

Her voice was hollow, her eyes distending. The bitterness in her throat burned like acid. In her head, thoughts tumbled like falling rocks. Each one smashing into her.

That's all I was to him—all the value I had. Less than a handful of shares in his precious hotel chain! And for that—for nothing more than that—he agreed to marry another woman. Thinking I'd go along with it.

Pain knifed through her.

'You traded me for a handful of shares!' She hurled the words at him again, her face convulsing now. '*That* was why you put me through what you did! You agreed to *marry* someone for *that*?'

That tic came again in his cheek. 'As you say,' he said tightly.

She stared at him. 'How *could* you, Vito? How could you stoop that low? With all your wealth, to want yet more—to be prepared to *marry* for it! Stringing me along while you did so, making a fool of me—bringing me to Rome right under the nose of the woman you were going to marry? And you *really* think that coming here and telling me all that to my face is going to make me change my mind about you?'

There was derision in her voice, open scorn. Raw anger. She had to put it there—because only that could quench that phosphorus flare of hope and longing.

He moved restlessly. There was about him an air of withdrawal, as if he'd shut himself inside himself. His eyes had blanked now—there was nothing in them, no emotion…nothing. He picked up the magazine page, lying abandoned on the tabletop, folded it mechanically, and slipped it into his breast pocket.

Then he looked across at Eloise again. 'I've said what I came to say, Eloise,' he said. 'I've sought you out to say it—to explain to you why I behaved as I did. And,' he went on, and now his voice was weighted down as if with lead, 'for one other reason.'

He looked at her, and there was a bleakness in his eyes now that had not been there till this moment. A draining of hope.

'I sought you out because I needed to know, Eloise, just what we had come to mean to each other. To discover if…if there could have been anything more to us than a summer romance.' His expression twisted. 'When we arrived in Rome all I wanted was to focus on you! But—'

She cut across him, her voice scathing, bitter. 'But the little business of your *marriage* got in the way! So then I just turned into a prospective mistress, didn't I? To be neatly stashed away in a love nest in Amalfi!'

Vito's hand slashed through the air. 'No! It was never that! *Never.* I just wanted—'

'You wanted to get hold of some shares. Yes, you said.'

Eloise's voice was harsh, grating. Her eyes as hard as stones. She couldn't bear this. Couldn't bear to have Vito saying such words to her. Vito who had callously set her aside for the sake of some extra shares…

But you could have him back! You could have him back right now—all you have to say to him is that you want him. Need him in your life. And that it's not just you who needs him.

Temptation, overpowering and overwhelming, hovered in front of her.

I could have the dream! I could have Vito in my life... in my future. Making a family with me.

But then, like cold acidic water, came the knowledge that it was impossible. He was not a man whose values and choices she would ever want to understand. Not a man she would inflict on anyone, let alone—

She took a shuddering breath, her mind shearing away from the future that must be hers, and hers alone, with no one to share it with her. She made her voice indifferent.

'Look, Vito—forget it. You made your choice—those shares were more important to you than I was. Well, they can stay that way.'

She took a step backwards. Claws were ripping into her, shredding her.

For one long moment he looked at her, his face unreadable, closed. Expressionless except for one tic high in his cheek, the pressure of his set jaw.

'I'll go,' he said. His voice was staccato. Terse. Infinitely distant. 'I apologise for disturbing you like this, and you have my assurance that I will make no further attempt to communicate with you. I accept that our time together is...gone. That there is nothing left between us. The fault for that is mine entirely. Goodbye, Eloise.'

He turned away, walked back towards the door of the library, every line of his body rigid as he disappeared from her view.

The claws inside her tore again, and her throat was as tight as drawn wire. For a single agonising second she wanted to hurl herself forward, catch at his shoulder, throw herself into his arms...

Beg him not to go.

But she would not let herself.

Somewhere beyond she was dimly aware of the sound of a car's engine, and the scrunch of gravel beyond the library windows. She heard footsteps cross the hall, heard a murmur of Italian—presumably him speaking to Maria or Giuseppe—and then the sound of the front door opening. Dimly, in part of her consciousness, she was aware of conversation in English, of another male voice, one with an American accent. The other voice, low-pitched, was Vito's, but then it was cut off by the closing of the front door.

And still she could not move.

Then suddenly, abruptly, there was more noise out in the hallway and the chatter of a youthful voice, and a moment later Johnny erupted into the library, rushing up to her.

'Daddy's home! He's come home to play with me! We're going swimming!'

Eloise jerked to life, like a statue animated. 'That's lovely,' she said, but her response was mechanical.

Beyond the window she saw a flash of red, heard a throaty, familiar roar fading into the distance down the driveway.

'Daddy!' Johnny did an about-turn, seeing his father in the doorway. 'Swimming! Swimming!' he shouted excitedly.

'Swimming it is,' said his father with a grin. Then his eyes went to Eloise, their expression changing. 'Well, well, you're a dark horse, Nanny Ellie! Vito Viscari, no less! That's some beau to have!' He grinned down at his son. 'Of course if you were Junior, here, his main attraction would be that very neat Ferrari he's just roared off in—Johnny was trying to persuade Giuseppe to let him get into the driving seat.'

'Vroom-vroom!' chirped Johnny in happy agreement, and ran around the room as if steering a car.

'But I suspect,' John Carldon went on, addressing Eloise once more, with an amused look open in his face, 'that for you it's more likely to be the film star looks that a totally unfair Providence has heaped upon him! Laura will be mad as fire that she missed him!'

The amused look deepened.

'Maybe, now that she knows he's...ah...coming calling,' he went on, 'she'll snap him up for a dinner party. Oh, and, of course,' he went on blithely, 'if you need time off to head into Manhattan now that he's Stateside, just let us know. Presumably he stays at the Viscari when he's in New York?'

He frowned suddenly. 'Or maybe not. It's not a Viscari Hotel any more, is it? That was one of the ones that went over to Falcone.'

He shook his head, not seeming to notice that his son's nanny had frozen.

'Bad business, that,' he went on, his voice sombre now. 'And pretty tough on the guy—seeing half his inheritance wiped out, just like that. It made quite a stir in the financial press—even over here. Half the entire company was sold over Viscari's head by his uncle's widow to his biggest rival. Nic Falcone has scooped up a real treasure pot—taken his pick of the prime locations. A blow that heavy will take some recovering from. But Viscari'll do it, I'm sure. I can't see him not fighting back. Trying to rebuild everything that's been ripped from him.'

His expression changed, and the glint was back in his eye.

'Of course he'll be here for other reasons, too, won't he? Other attractions!' He grinned at her.

But Eloise did not smile back. Could not. Could not move a muscle. Could only hear her employer continue talking as he caught his son's hand to stop his peregrinations.

'Hotels aren't my usual investment sector, but if Laura gets her dinner party I'll make sure some of the guests are useful to him. After all,' he said teasingly, 'if Vito Viscari's your beau we should keep him sweet. We don't want to lose you before we have to!'

His expression changed again, and he glanced down at his son, who was tugging on his hand.

'OK... OK, Junior—no need to pull my hand off. Swimming it is—see you later, Nanny Ellie.'

He headed off, Johnny still tugging at him excitedly, chattering away.

Slowly, very slowly, Eloise turned away, walking up the stairs back to the nursery quarters on legs that did not seem to be hers any more.

Vito opened the throttle, letting the powerful engine roar. Wanting the noise to drown out everything that was knifing through him. The bitter, bitter taste of total defeat.

I should never have sought her out! Never!

Because to have seen her again, to have his gaze rest on her in the flesh, not just in his memories, had opened the floodgates within him!

He had spent all those precious weeks in Europe with her, wondering if he dared believe she could be the one woman in the world he could fall in love with. He had spent these last brutally grim weeks missing her with an intensity that was like a knife in his guts.

Finally finding her, seeing her, had been like a brand on his flesh. Making everything crystal-clear to him.

Emotion had surged within him. He had been desperate to get her to understand why he had done what he had. Desperate to win her back.

But it had been a disaster—a catastrophe. Smashing his hopes to pieces.

Did I really expect more?

He railed at himself, his grip tightening on the wheel of the car.

Did I really expect her just to fall straight back into my arms as if the past nightmare months had never happened?

He should have known better. Should have realised how impossible that was.

In his head her scathing accusation rang again.

'You traded me for a handful of shares!'

His hands clenched again around the wheel.

Dio, I messed up from beginning to end! And I've lost everything I wanted to keep—everything!

Bleakness seared across his mind as he faced what he'd done, what he'd lost. He'd wanted to keep Eloise in his life—discover exactly what she meant to him—and now he'd lost her for ever. She'd made that clear enough! He'd wanted to keep his promise to his dying father—and he'd broken it. He'd wanted to keep the Viscari legacy intact—and he'd had it smashed it to pieces.

It's all been for nothing—less than nothing... I betrayed Eloise's trust in me and I've betrayed my father's trust in me.

He drove on, filled with bleakness and despair. He would leave New York tonight...fly down to Ste Cecile. That hotel, at least, was still his, for Nic Falcone already had a strong existing presence in the Caribbean, and wasn't interested in the Viscari project there—though he'd helped himself to the pick of the rest of the Viscari North American portfolio. Including the uber-prestigious Viscari Manhattan.

Out of loyalty to his former manager there, Vito was staying in his usual suite—though every sign of the Falcone rebranding was like a whiplash across his shoulders.

But I can't give in—and I will not go under!

His jaw steeled, eyes hardening. If Falcone was mopping up existing Viscari Hotels—well, there would be *new* Viscari Hotels opened. It would take time, but time was something he would have a great deal of now. So much gaping time to fill...

Time to rebuild his legacy. Restore what he had lost.

Pain sliced through him again, severing his flesh. What else could he do now? What else was left for him?

Her name cried through his head like a fleeing ghost.

Eloise! What use was it to find you and lose you all over again...?

Fool! Fool that he had been! To hope for her forgiveness—her understanding.

To hope for reunion...

'Mum, I need your help.' Eloise's voice was urgent as she spoke on the phone from her room at the Carldons'. 'Can I stay at your apartment tonight? I *have* to go and see Vito this evening.'

'Vito?' Her mother's voice sharpened down the line. 'Eloise, do *not* tell me he's the waste-of-space Italian you got so disastrously involved with—'

Eloise's throat tightened. She had never told her mother Vito's identity, and her mother had never asked—had specifically told her that, given Eloise's decision, she had no need to know, and that it was irrelevant anyway.

'Yes,' she admitted grittily. 'Vito Viscari. He found out where I was working and—'

Again her mother interrupted her, in her usual forthright manner. 'Viscari? As in... Viscari Hotels?'

'Yes,' said Eloise.

She did *not* want an inquisition about Vito's identity. All she wanted right now was her mother's help in a very practical way. But her mother's attention had snapped on Vito's name.

'Vito Viscari! Good grief! I had no idea.' There was

open surprise in her voice. Then her tone changed. 'Why are you meeting him?' she asked sharply.

'I… I have to talk to him,' Eloise got out.

'Well, make sure that's all you do! This is *no* time for rushing into anything! You've been quite rash enough as it is—'

She broke off, and Eloise could hear a voice in the background. Then her mother was back on the line, her voice crisp and brisk.

'Eloise, I have to go now. Let yourself into the apartment—I'll be working late.'

She rang off. Slowly, Eloise replaced the handset. Emotion was roiling within her. Phoning her mother had been the *easy* phone call to make…

With slightly shaking fingers she dialled the number for the Viscari Manhattan. He *would* be staying there—wouldn't he?

But it isn't even his hotel any more…

She felt a stab in her stomach. That stab came again as the voice down the line intoned, 'Falcone Manhattan—how may I direct your call?'

She made herself focus on what had to be done, and left the message she had to leave.

'My name is Eloise Dean. Please tell Mr Viscari, when he arrives back at the hotel, that I urgently need to see him. I'm coming into Manhattan tonight and will be at the hotel at eight.'

It was all she could bring herself to say. All she could bring herself to hope.

CHAPTER SEVEN

TENSION WAS RACING through Vito. Was he insane to put himself through this for a second time in one day? He'd been intending to head straight for JFK, ready to take the next flight to the Caribbean as if all the hounds of hell were tearing at his heels.

And now—

Now he was waiting in the elegant bar of the hotel that had once been his but was no longer, with a dry martini in front of him, doing his damnedest to steady his nerves. Watching the entrance like a hawk.

Eight o'clock, the message had said. It was five past now. Would she come at all? And why was she coming?

He felt emotion spike in him, and clamped down on it.

I'd hoped so much, pinned so much on telling her what I wasn't able to tell her in Rome...and it made no difference to her at all.

He remained unforgiven.

A sense of bitter irony assailed him. All his life women had come easily to him. His looks, his charm, his wealth, his social position—all had meant that his love-life had been sunny, plentiful, effortless. Any woman he'd smiled at had responded to him. Including Eloise.

Did I expect Eloise to be like all the other women? So keen on me that she would snap me up again after a simple apology?

He frowned. No, that had not been it. It had been because he'd longed for her to forgive him—to accept him back in her life.

The searing sense of loss he'd felt when she'd fled from Rome came again, with double intensity. A humourless smile thinned his mouth. He'd questioned himself as to what Eloise meant to him. Well, losing her had shown him, hadn't it? Losing her not once, but twice…

And the bitterest truth of all was that it had only taken setting eyes on her again this afternoon for him to know, with blazing clarity, that *she*, of all the women in the world, was the one who meant most to him. The time dividing them had vanished in an instant, and he'd known that everything he'd desired her for was still blazingly true. He wanted her—and she was still lost to him.

Unless her coming here tonight means…

No, he must not hope. He'd hoped before, and had had his hope smashed to pieces. Better—safer—to finish his martini and steel himself for seeing her again.

Maybe for the last time ever…

He lifted his glass, but it froze halfway to his lips.

She was there, in the entrance, and her eyes were fixed on him.

Eloise's eyes went to Vito immediately. He was sitting at the bar. Slowly, she walked towards him. His expression had become masked as he'd seen her, and she felt emotion swirl within her, troubling and troubled. But she tried to set them aside. She was here for one purpose only. To say the words she must say. *Unsay* what she had thrown at him so angrily. So unfairly.

'You traded me for a handful of shares!'

Only it had not been a handful, had it? It had been the severing of his legacy—an entire half of it handed to his rival.

'Hello, Vito,' she said.

Her voice sounded strange...far away. She looked at him, but could not quite meet his eyes. Or perhaps it was his eyes not meeting hers.

She swallowed. 'Thank you for seeing me.'

His expression shifted minutely. 'I was en route to JFK,' he said. He moved his martini glass, gestured to the stool at the bar beside his. 'What is it that you want to say?'

His expression was wary, cutting her off from him. She perched herself on the stool, setting her handbag on the bar, taking a breath.

'I didn't realise,' she said, 'just what those shares meant. Johnny's father told me—he assumed I knew. He told me...told me you'd lost half of the Viscari Hotels.' She took another breath. 'I'm so sorry, Vito.' Her voice was small. She made herself go on. 'So sorry that I made it sound so...trivial. I didn't know. Didn't realise.' She swallowed. 'Didn't understand.'

The barman had glided up to them, hovering attentively, knowing full who Vito was even if he no longer owned the hotel.

Vito went into courtesy mode. 'What would you like to drink?' he asked Eloise.

There was nothing more in his voice than there would have been if she were a minor acquaintance.

She hesitated. A thousand memories pierced like needles under her skin. Once she would have said, *Oh, a Bellini would be lovely!* But now she dared not. And not just because of the memories.

'OJ, please— and water,' she said, and the barman nodded, and glided away again.

Unwillingly, Eloise registered that his uniform was now emblazoned with the Falcone logo—so was the drinks menu, and the bar mats, and anything else that had writing on it. Vito's rival had branded his new possessions as his own. Slamming home to her what had been taken from Vito...

There was an awkward silence, and Eloise knew she must speak again. Made herself do so. 'If...if you'd married your step-cousin, would you have lost the hotels?'

He shook his head. Tersely he answered, 'No. Marlene—my uncle's widow—would have handed me the shares after the wedding. That was her plan. Her way of getting me to marry her daughter, Carla.'

Eloise frowned. 'But why...?' She paused while the barman set up her drinks, then moved away. 'Why did she want you to marry her daughter? Why did Carla want to marry *you*? Was she in love with you?'

Was *that* why Carla had raged? Because of raging, furious jealousy?

But Vito was shaking her head. 'No, she was in love with another man—who'd just dumped her to marry another woman.'

A hiss escaped Eloise and her eyes widened with disbelief. The irony of what Vito had just said...

He was speaking again. 'I was to be her...her facesaver, I guess.' His voice twisted. 'Even if the only way she could make me do it was through her mother's bribe.'

Eloise was silent a moment, absorbing what Vito had said—and the bitter irony of his step-cousin reaching for him to assuage her pride, thereby causing Eloise's own galling humiliation at Vito's deceit. Then she reached for her orange juice, drank it down.

She spoke again—asked the question she had to ask. 'Vito, if you'd already made the decision to accept that... that bribe, to marry Carla and get your uncle's shares, what made you think it was acceptable to start a relationship with *me*?'

There was harshness in her voice, and she heard it—

but it was justified. Above everything, that was the one
thing he could not defend.

But he was staring at her. 'Eloise... Marlene dropped
her bombshell the first evening we got to Rome!'

Shock ripped through Eloise. 'You agreed to marry
Carla *that night*?'

Violently, Vito shook his head. 'No! I told them it was
insanity and walked out!'

Coldness pooled in her stomach. 'Yet the very next day
you were trying to bundle me out of sight to Amalfi! Obviously you'd changed your mind about Carla by then—
and decided to keep me as your convenient mistress!'

'No! Eloise—how can you *think* that? How *can* you?'
He took a ragged breath. 'I just wanted you out of Rome—
away from all the...the complications.'

He drained the last of his martini. Agitation possessed
him—adrenaline was surging, and yet being reigned in
simultaneously. Just having Eloise there, so close—so
far—was a torment. And to what purpose?

*When she's asked me all her questions she'll go. She'll
still go. And I'll still be on my way to JFK...never to see
her again...*

'Out of Rome till *when*, Vito?' she was demanding.
'And what *for*? You were going to *marry* Carla!' There
was a lash of anger in her voice now, and derision too.
What the hell would the point have been of her staying
down in Amalfi?

His eyes were on her. Like lead weights. 'No,' he said.
'I had no intention of marrying her.'

Eloise's face contorted. She had wanted to be calm,
yet emotion was jumping inside her, replaying the nightmare of that scene in Rome. 'Vito, you said to my face
that you were her fiancé!'

The line of his jaw was taut. 'I said it to get her out of
there. To...placate her.' The memory of that hideous mo-

ment was like magma in his head. 'I needed her to believe I was going to go through with her mother's scheming.' He reached for his martini glass, but it was empty. 'I just needed *time*.'

'Why?' Eloise demanded in a hollow voice. Whatever Machiavellian games Vito had played, they sickened her. First rejecting Marlene Viscari's bribe, and then appearing to accept it.

And trying to keep me on a string as well...

'Time for Carla to calm down. She was totally strung out—manic!—you could see that for yourself! Given time, I desperately hoped she'd realise that marrying me would not solve her problems—would only make her more miserable. And once she'd seen that her mother would have had to abandon her ludicrous hopes of our ever marrying. It would resign her either to finally agreeing to my offer to buy the shares from her at a handsome profit— as I have been trying to do—or remaining the sleeping partner she's been since Guido's death. Then, finally, I'd have been free to come back to you. Free to—'

He broke off.

How can I tell her here, now, when she is barely being civil to me, that I thought she might be the woman I was falling in love with?

She saw the veiling in his eyes, felt his withdrawal. It hurt like a splash of acid on her skin. There was so much distance between them—so much had parted them.

Including her own impetuous flight, and her refusal to listen to him. She had refused to give him time to explain that ugly scene. Had stormed out instead, denouncing him, judging him unheard. Compunction smote her.

He was speaking again, and she made herself listen.

'But after you'd left—disappeared—and made it totally clear that you wanted nothing more to do with me... He hesitated, then continued heavily, 'It seemed...less important to refuse Carla.' He took a sharp intake of razoring breath. 'So I agreed to marry her after all.'

His eyes flickered away, his jaw tightening.

'It seemed the fastest way to get the shares out of Marlene's clutches. Carla could have her glittering, face-saving wedding, but six months later she'd apply for an annulment on the grounds of non-consummation and we'd go our separate ways. I'd keep Guido's shares—and pay Carla a premium price for them.'

Eloise looked at him. 'You told me there was no wedding.'

'In the end I couldn't go through with it.'

Eloise's eyes were piercing. 'Why not?'

The silence stretched between them. She saw his hand clench on the surface of the bar, then relax forcibly.

'It would have been dishonourable,' he said eventually, in a low, strained voice He did not look at her while he spoke. Could not.

There was silence again. Thick, impenetrable. Eloise could feel a vein throbbing at her temple. She looked at Vito, letting her eyes rest on him, trying to see him clearly—not with the haze of heady romance that had bathed him while she was whisked from one European city to another, and not with the bitter anger she'd felt at his betrayal. A betrayal he had not intended, but had committed all the same.

Her eyes rested on a man prepared to marry a woman solely for financial advantage. Because he'd been bribed to marry her.

A man prepared to sell out, to put profit before people.

That was the taint in his character that would stain him for ever. Impossible to love such a man, to want to make a family with him...

Emotion stabbed at her again, and it made her voice harsh as she spoke again.

'You couldn't resist it, could you?' she said tautly. 'You imagined you could string Carla along, stash me away somewhere secretly for the duration, get hold of the shares, and come up smelling of roses!' Her voice filled with derision, lashing her own stupid hopes as well as him. 'Still, you turned the bribe down in the end, so at least your conscience is clear now!'

A laugh broke from Vito—harsh and brief. 'I hardly think so,' he said.

He caught the barman's eye—beckoned him over, ordered another martini. To hell with it—he was going to hell in a handcart here, and he might as well go there with another martini in him! It might numb him against the ride...

Eloise was frowning. 'What do you mean?' she demanded. 'You did the decent thing in the end, Vito—'

He turned towards her. His expression was savage now. '*Did* I? I'll go and tell that to my father's tombstone, shall I?'

She was staring at him. Staring at him with clear blue eyes—as clear as her conscience.

'What do you mean?' she said again. There was blankness in her voice. Incomprehension.

Vito seized the second martini as it was placed in front of him. It burned as he swallowed. Burned like the memory he did not want to remember. But which had forced itself into his head.

'Get the shares back, Vito, my son, my son! Any way you can—whatever the cost...pay any price...promise me—promise me!'

His father's breathless, stricken voice, his dying gasps...imploring him, begging him to promise.

Time sucked him back to the present and he slid his eyes away from the clear blue eyes gazing at him with incomprehension.

'When my father had his fatal heart attack,' he said, his voice dull, his gaze fixed on the way the green olive in his martini was speared—as *he* had been speared, 'I rushed to the hospital. The doctors said he had little time left. My mother was there—'

He broke off.

'It was...very bad. My father wanted to speak to me, say his last words to me. He...he begged me...made me promise that whatever it cost, whatever price I had to pay, I would get back the shares his brother had left to Marlene. He said I must not lose the legacy that four generations of our family had built up from nothing. I must not betray that. I must do whatever it took to get the shares back into Viscari possession. Keep them safe.'

His eyes darkened.

'That day—the day you left me...' he took another razoring breath '... Marlene threatened to sell her shareholding to Nic Falcone if I didn't immediately announce my engagement to her daughter.'

Eloise stared, shock ravaging through her. 'She did *what*?'

That wasn't a bribe—that was blackmail. Blatant, vicious blackmail. *Forcing his hand in the most ruthless way imaginable.*

Vito looked at her. His eyes were blank. 'That's why Carla confronted you—demanded I tell you I was her fiancé. And that,' he said, biting the words out viciously, 'was why I could not deny it. I had to *somehow* keep my promise to my father.'

He reached for his martini again. Took another burning slug.

'A promise I betrayed when I jilted Carla at the altar. Marlene sold the shares to Falcone that evening.' His expression twisted. 'So, no, my conscience is *not* clear—it never can be. *Never!* I can argue with myself all I like, say that I was right not to marry Carla, but it doesn't absolve me of breaking my promise to my dying father! *Nothing* can—'

He fell silent, hunched over his martini glass. Seeing before him only the contorted face of his father, hearing only the broken, stricken sobbing of his mother, feeling only the desperate, frail clutch of his father's failing grip on his arm as death swept over him and took him from his wife, his son, for ever.

And then, faintly, he was aware of another touch on his arm. A gentler one now. And a voice speaking.

'You gave this promise to your father on his deathbed?'

There was questioning in the voice now. But not accusation. Something else.

The voice was speaking again. 'Vito, is *that* why you agreed to Marlene's blackmail?' She would not call it a bribe any longer—it had not been a bribe. 'Because of that deathbed promise?'

His face convulsed. 'Why else?' His voice was as tight as wire pulled to breaking point. 'And now I've betrayed it—betrayed my father. Lost the hotels—broken my promise to him!'

The hand on his sleeve pressed, and he felt a warmth coming through the pressure.

'Vito—listen to me—*listen.*' There was an urgency in Eloise's voice now, as she spoke, but then she paused. She could not bear to see Vito like this—so...so stricken, so self-accusing.

I have to make this right—I got it wrong, yet again! And now I have to make it right. For Vito's sake—

And for more than his sake? No—no time for that now. No time for speculation or thinking about herself. Or thinking about—

She cut her thoughts off, focusing on this moment alone.

'Listen to me,' she said again.

She saw him about to lift the martini glass and stayed him with her other hand, letting it close over his. Letting the touch of his fingers under hers surge like an electric current through her. He turned his head to look at her, and his stricken eyes made her throat tighten.

'You should not have had to make that promise,' she said. She took a breath, ragged in her lungs. 'Because...' she took another breath, her eyes fastening on his '...this situation is not of your making. *Or* your father's! Aren't you forgetting one tiny little detail? It was your *uncle* who chose to leave his shares to his widow! Whatever his reasons for doing so, *he* has to take the responsibility for what has happened now! This hotel—' she gestured around her '—and half of the rest of them now belong to your rival—well, that's *his* doing, not *yours*.' She took a steadying breath. 'Don't you see that, Vito?'

He was staring at her, frowningly. As if what she had said made no sense. She had to *make* him see it. So she plunged on, emotion streaming through her.

'Vito, tell me—tell me right now: if your father hadn't extracted that terrible deathbed promise out of you would you have entertained for one moment Marlene's blackmail?'

He shook his head, his mouth tightening to a grim line. 'No,' he said.

It was as if a garrotte around her throat had loosened, and she felt the blood flow through her veins again, rich and warming. Releasing so much from her. She gave a long, slow exhalation, her eyes never leaving his.

Her expression changed, thoughts crowding into her head. Maybe Vito's father had been dying, but he'd placed a burden on his son that had almost destroyed him. Crippled him with unnecessary guilt.

Her eyes hardened. Hadn't her own father done the

same? Making her think all through her childhood that if only she'd been a boy he would not have abandoned her?

Vito's voice cut across her familiar darkening thoughts.

'Do you...do you really mean what you said about it being my uncle's responsibility, not mine?' He spoke as if he could not bring himself to believe what she had said. Did not dare to believe it.

'Yes!' she replied immediately, without the slightest hesitation, and with vehemence in her tone.

He felt her hand squeeze tightly over his, reinforcing the vehemence of her voice.

'Didn't he think his widow might use her ownership of his share of the hotels malignly?'

Vito was silent a moment. 'I think,' he said slowly, 'that he hoped it might make us...my parents, myself...accept Marlene more. Maybe,' he said, and the words were being dragged from him now, 'if we'd been more...welcoming to her, she wouldn't have felt she had to... I don't know... prove she was part of the family in her obsession with me marrying her daughter.'

'Vito—don't think about it any more. It's over—it's gone. Don't let it haunt you any more—please!'

She took a breath, then paused, her face working. Part of her, somewhere inside her head, was thinking how strange it was that she should be here, comforting Vito. Yet it felt right too. *So* right.

There was something else she needed to say. Something she had to acknowledge.

'Vito—' She took a breath, knowing she needed to say what she had to say *now.* 'Now...now that I understand what was actually going on—not just what you did about Carla, but *why*—and what the whole grim, ghastly situation was, and the horrendous pressure you were under to sort out a mess which was *nothing* to do with you, I know...' She swallowed. 'I know I have been...unfair on you. I judged you too harshly. And…and I'm sorry, Vito! I'm truly sorry—'

She broke off, her voice twisting, not able to say more. A heaviness was crushing her. Emotions were roiling. Emotions she did not want to think about—not now. They were too much…

Gently, she felt him squeeze her fingers.

'And I,' said Vito, his voice low, intent, 'am truly sorry too.' His voice changed. 'If I could take back time—do it differently—I would have told you sooner. Explained the situation. '

His expression was changing. If he had done that— if Eloise had said to him in Rome what she had said to him now…

If she had shown me that it was not up to my father, or to me, to sort out what Guido had done! Not at the price I had to pay for it!

And though it haunted him still—not going through with the promise he'd made his father in order to set his mind at rest—he knew that Eloise had set him free from the guilt that had consumed him since he had walked away from Carla. His eyes rested on Eloise. There was gratitude in his face, and wonder, too, that it was the woman he had wronged who had given him this gift now.

Instinctively, without thinking, only knowing it was an imperative he could not halt, he turned her fingers in his, lifted them to his mouth, brushed them with his lips after a dip of his head towards her.

'Thank you,' he said. Softly. Gratefully.

He felt her hand tremble in his, felt her slip her fingers free, saw her clutch at her glass, busy herself with taking a gulp.

'I'm sorry—I should not have—' He broke off, contrite.

Her eyes flared back to his, her head shaking. 'No— *I'm* sorry—' She took a breath. 'Vito—'

She couldn't say any more. The brush of his lips on her hand was quivering in her head, and she could feel her heart-rate quicken. She swallowed, looked away, set down her glass.

Vito was speaking again, saying her name.

'Eloise—' He stopped abruptly. His brow furrowed, uncertainty flickering in his eyes.

She saw him take a breath. Her quickened heart-rate was not slowing down. The room seemed hot suddenly, despite the cooling chill of the air-conditioning.

'Eloise—' He said her name again. 'Tell me—if you want me to go, leave you alone now, for me to go back to Italy, then I'll do so. I'll take the first flight out and I won't trouble you again.' He paused, and it was as if his eyes were pouring into hers now. 'But if...if you think that maybe there's something left...something of what we had...something that can become—'

'Become what, Vito?'

She found her throat dry suddenly—so, so dry. Emotions were scissoring inside her. It had been so easy to hate Vito—so easy to condemn him for what he'd done to her, to write him out of her life, her future.

But now... Seeing him this afternoon, for the first time in so long, she had been in a state of absolute turmoil, shredded inside with conflicting emotions that seemed to contradict each other, override each other, cancel each other out. But she had found no resolution. None.

I've forgiven him for what he did, and yet—

A sense of wariness possessed her. Once, in a different lifetime, she had given herself to Vito, rushed off with him to whirl her way through a haze of carefree weeks, soaring in new-found ecstasy with him. But then she had crashed and burned. And her life now was totally different—changed completely for ever. A new future awaited her—one that she must bend all her powers to in order to get it right, bringing responsibilities she could never abandon. She could no longer afford to be impulsive...

I have to be careful this time—I have to be!

She felt wariness claw at her again, but even as it did she felt her heart beating faster as she gazed at him, drinking in everything about him the way she always had... from the feathered sable of his hair, to his long, ink-dark eyelashes, the beautiful line of his mouth, the elegant length of his hands, the superb cut of the bespoke designer suit sheathing the lean, muscled body that she knew so intimately...

She felt the rush of her blood, felt heat curl in her body. Her heart cried out to him.

Vito—oh, Vito—how much I've missed you!

But she had to fight it down –she *had* to! She couldn't just succumb, as she had at that first fateful moment of falling at his feet.

I can't do that again. I can't. I mustn't. Too much is at stake—far too much.

He was speaking, and she made herself listen, dragged herself out of the swirling confusion in her head.

'I don't know, Eloise,' Vito said. 'I don't know—but I want to find out. That's why I came—why I had to find you.' He swallowed. 'At the very least you had to know *why* I'd done what I had. I owed you the truth, even if it changes nothing.'

She shook her head, negating his fear. 'But the truth— the real truth—*does* change things, Vito. It changes so much—'

His eyes were holding hers, intent, questioning. 'But does it change enough?'

She slid her gaze away. 'I don't know.'

They were his own words, echoed back.

Just for the briefest moment she felt the touch of his fingers on her hand, as it lay inert on the bar-top.

'Perhaps,' he said quietly, 'we might try and find out.'

He shifted position, leant towards her slightly. There was a quickening in his voice as he spoke.

'Eloise, would you have dinner with me? Just dinner. Here—now. Just so we can... I don't know...talk things through, maybe? Or maybe *not* talk them through. Maybe just have a companionable meal together? See how we get on? I won't pressure you—you have my word. And besides...' He looked at her now. 'Pressure is the *last* thing we need now—either of us.' He took a breath. 'So, what do you say?'

There was a diffidence in his voice, an uncertainty. It struck her that never had Vito *ever* sounded uncertain before. Unsure of her response.

But he always knew what my response was going to be, didn't he? He knew I'd just acquiesce instantly, totally! Go along with everything he said, everything he wanted!

A poodle—that was what her plain-speaking mother had called her. Jumping up eagerly every time he said, *Walkies!* He hadn't been arrogant about it, or demanding, but she'd always gone along with him in everything. She'd kept telling herself to be careful, but in the end she hadn't been careful at all, had she?

But now?

What was the truth of it? What was the truth of how she felt about Vito? How could she know?

All she knew was that she had to find out. Because now, with the future she was facing, it was essential for her to make the right decision about Vito—about what she meant to him and he to her.

And what he would feel when he—

No, that was too far, too fast. For now this was about themselves, only that. That was what she must first discover.

So, slowly, she nodded her head. Saw his eyes flare

with relief, with gladness. Felt a little lift inside her in response.

He lifted a hand, had the barman scurrying over to him.

'We'll be dining here,' he said. 'We'd like the menu, please.'

A minute later the maître d' glided out of the restaurant, greeting Vito with respectful familiarity, assuring him that standards were every bit as high now, despite… He grimaced, left it at that. Being tactful about the change in ownership.

Five minutes on and they were seated at their table, their choices for dining made. A strange, powerful sense of familiarity encompassed her as she sat across the table from Vito—as she had sat a hundred times, in a score of Viscari Hotels across Europe. Yet again she felt emotions tumble about inside her head, jumbling the past and the present. So familiar—and yet utterly changed.

But it feels good to be here with him…

Emotion flickered like a candle in her head, casting light and shadows.

It feels…right.

She veered away from the thought again, knowing with a steadying breath that above all she must be careful… cautious. The day had brought so much turmoil to her…

She took another little steadying breath. Vito was right—they needed calm. That was it. Calmness, ordinariness. Ease…

No pressure. No pressure at all.

She felt herself steady and the candle ceased to flicker, burning calmly instead.

When the chosen wine arrived, instinctively Eloise moved to cover her glass. She sensed Vito's eyes, curious on her, and gave an awkward smile.

'Empty calories,' she said, knowing she must give a

reason. Then, with sudden decision, she took her hand away, let the sommelier fill her glass. Half a glass would not hurt her.

She felt Vito's eyes on her, warm now, and was aware that his gaze was sweeping over her figure. It filled her with self-consciousness, and she was glad her top was as loosely cut as it was, despite her gain in weight being only slight.

'You look beautiful,' he said, his voice as warm as his gaze.

Eloise felt colour stain her cheeks. 'Don't—' she said. It was half a whisper, half a plea.

Immediately his expression changed. 'I'm sorry—I have no right—'

She shook her head. 'No—no, it's not that. Please, I'm sorry— I—'

He held up a hand. 'We'll keep this light,' he said. 'No pressure, I said, and I meant it.' His eyes were soft with humour, half-rueful, half-conspiratorial.

Her own gaze softened. 'Thank you,' she said. The flare of colour faded and she took a mouthful of wine. The chilled crisp Chablis tasted so good, and she set the glass down with appreciation and regret. Even without her own compelling reason to avoid alcohol, drinking too quickly like this with Vito was the last thing she needed. She needed to keep her senses set to 'sensible'.

She watched him take a mouthful himself, then look across at her. Saw him take a deliberate breath.

'So,' he said, 'how did you end up with that little bundle of energy, young Johnny, to look after?'

The humour was uppermost in his voice now, and Eloise gratefully followed his lead. Clearly he wanted to talk about things that were not imbued with deep, heavy emotions, with no troubling memories of a past that had gone so wrong. No pressure, he had said, and she was glad of it.

'It was a contact through my mother,' she said. 'She knew the Carldons were looking for a new nanny and put me forward.'

'Your mother lives in New York?'

'Yes, in Manhattan. She works downtown. I'm staying at her apartment tonight.'

Why had she said that? Was it to let him know not to have any expectations? What was she *thinking* of, entertaining such a thought? She focused hurriedly on what he was saying in reply.

His glance flickered towards her. 'I didn't know she was American,' he said.

Eloise shook her head. 'She isn't—she's British. Or at least she was *born* British. Maybe she's taken US citizenship by now—I don't know.' She gave a slight shrug. 'We don't communicate a great deal now—not that we ever did, really.'

She could not hide the sardonic tinge to her voice as she said that.

Vito heard it, and wondered, but did not follow through. *No pressure*, he'd promised, and he would keep his promise. So all he said was, 'If I'd known she lived in New York I guess I'd have tried to find you that way first.' He paused a moment. His eyes on her still, but slightly veiled. 'You never told me—'

She met his gaze head-on. '*You* never told *me* about your aunt having half the Viscari shares and holding them over your head.'

For a moment Vito didn't answer. Then he said slowly, 'We never really talked much about our families, did we?'

She bowed her head. 'No, we didn't.'

There was a silence. Vito took another mouthful of wine. Strange emotions were building in him, but he wanted to disperse them. He didn't want things getting heavy—not again.

Deliberately he lightened his voice as he set down his glass. Reverting to a safer subject. 'Young Johnny's definitely a cute kid,' he said, his voice upbeat now. 'And he definitely likes cars!'

'Especially fast ones,' Eloise answered dryly, following his lead and grateful to do so. She felt as if they were skating on paper-thin ice, and right now she wanted the security of dry land. Easy subjects. 'His father owns quite a few.'

'John Carldon...' Vito mused, recalling the brief introductory exchange with Eloise's employer earlier that day. 'Is that the banking Carldons?'

'Oh, yes,' answered Eloise, even more dryly.

She paused. Should she say this? There were overwhelming reasons not to—but powerful ones to do so.

Conflict swirled in her. Then she spoke. 'He...he mentioned to me that...that maybe you'd like to come over some time. He said he'd see to it that there were people invited who might be...ah..."useful" to you. You know—about the hotels, what's happened to them...'

Vito smiled, slightly in surprise. 'That's good of him,' he said. 'My task for the next few years is going to be raising finance for expansion. It can't be fast, obviously, but I have to show the world that Viscari Hotels may be down, but I'm far from out.'

There was grimness in his voice, a resolution that Eloise could not be deaf to.

'Can you do it?' she asked tentatively.

Vito looked at her. 'Yes,' he said. There was no hesitation in his answer—not the slightest. 'And,' he went on, and the note of resolution was even more pronounced, 'I will do it with a lot less weight on my shoulders—a lot less self-inflicted guilt, thanks to you.'

His eyes went to her, softened.

'Eloise, thank you—thank you for what you said to

me. You've made it possible for me to look ahead instead of looking back.' He shook his head. 'I can't undo what my uncle did...' He eyed her with mixed emotion. 'And I do still feel conflicted about the promise I made my father and the circumstances of it. But I also know that there is enough of my grandfather and my great-grand-father who founded Viscari Hotels in me to mean that I can, with patience and determination, get things back to what they were. Falcone won't get the better of me! I won't let him!'

His voice changed, lightened.

'And if your boss is happy for me to talk investment with him and his contacts, I'd be delighted to accept any social invitation he names!' His eyes rested on her, wariness in them. 'Would that be all right with you, though, Eloise? I wouldn't want to impose my company on you.' Vito was frowning. 'I don't want to cause any awkward-ness,' he said.

'You won't,' she assured him, realising what he meant. 'The Carldons are very easy-going. And I guess Johnny might be allowed to mingle for a short time—just to check out all the guests' cars, you understand!' she said hu-morously. Then, daringly, in the same humorous voice, she went on. 'While all the female guests check *you* out, Vito!' she said mischievously. 'Laura Carldon is already sighing over you!'

He laughed, but there was a questioning look in his face now. 'And what about *you*, Eloise?'

His eyes, so deep, so dark, searched hers, and she felt their power, felt a wash of weakness go through her—a wash of longing.

She felt the colour flush her cheeks and she tore her eyes away. But she could not tear her ears away.

'You know I have eyes only for you—and all my sigh-ing will be for *you*, Eloise.'

Her gaze flew back to his, met it and mingled. She seemed to feel her heart stop in her chest. 'Vito—please, I—I...'

'I've missed you so much—'

There was a hollowness in his voice now. He moved to reach for her hand. He could not help himself.

Would she have let him take it? He did not find out—waiters were gliding up to them, serving their first course. Maybe it was good that they were—maybe it was good that it meant she did not have to answer him.

Instead, as they were left to themselves again, Vito made himself start another innocuous line of conversation—something anodyne about New York and all its frenetic busyness.

I promised her no pressure—just an easy evening, easy dining. Nothing more than that.

But even as he made himself remember that he could feel emotion coursing through him. Feel hope flaring. Desire kindling.

But was desire enough?

What is she to me? Be careful, Vito, he warned himself. *You came here to discover that, and when she rejected you again you were about to part with her for ever. So just because now she has softened towards you, don't just tumble down into being blinded by her beauty! You can't afford to get this wrong again.*

They were words he had to keep reminding himself of as the meal progressed. With deliberate effort he kept the conversation away from anything that might be heavy. And as the time went by he felt the tension ebbing away from him, little by little. Felt himself relax and slip back into the kind of easy companionship that they had always had.

At one point he even found himself leaning back, lifting his wine glass and saying, 'Do you remember, in Barcelona, when—?'

Whatever the recollection was, it seemed to come naturally, and she answered just as readily, capping it with another from a different city—one of so many they had visited in their weeks together as they'd toured the Viscari Hotels of Europe. He laughed at what she'd said, and felt a kind of gladness washing through him.

She was relaxing before his eyes, her gaze mingling easily with his, her smile ready, her conversation eager, enthusiastic. As if the time separating them had never been...

'Coffee?' Vito's enquiry came with the lazy lift of an eyebrow.

Eloise gave a replete sigh, glancing at her watch. Did she have time for coffee? Her eyes went back to Vito. She didn't want to leave now.

It feels good to be with him—so good!

Emotion caught in her throat but she suppressed it—and the memories that went with it.

'Do you have to go?'

Vito's voice brought her back to the present, and with a little start, a flush in her cheeks, she shook her head. 'Not quite yet,' she said.

They ordered coffee, and Eloise was conscious that she was lingering over it. Conscious, too, of Vito sitting opposite her, his gaze on her. Their conversation was desultory now as, little by little, breath by breath, she felt the atmosphere change between them. Charge and thicken.

He signed the bill, thanked the staff for their meal, then brought his gaze back to Eloise. She was sitting there, poised, two lines of colour running across her cheeks, flushed—and not just with the half-glass of wine she'd drunk. Her beauty overwhelmed her, drowned his senses.

His eyes met hers. He could no longer resist saying what was burning in him. 'I would ask you to stay,' he said, his voice low, husky. 'But I said no pressure. And you had my word on that. Although for all that...' He shook his head, as if there was nothing he could do about it. 'For all that, I cannot deny what I would ask of you had I not given you that promise.'

She saw him draw breath, felt the force of his eyes pouring into hers, felt the heat in her cheeks, and she was unable to tear her gaze from him as he held it with his, so effortlessly, as he had from the very first...

'I can't...' she breathed. 'I mustn't.'

He looked at her still. 'I know,' he said. The husk was still in his voice, but there was regret too. 'It would not be...wise.'

He shut his eyes for a moment, as if to recover his senses. Then opened them again. A different expression was in them now.

'Eloise—everything went wrong for us in Rome. When we arrived all I wanted was time with you, to get to know you, explore our feelings. But time was what we never had together there. So...' He took a breath, his eyes intent, focused on her totally. 'Maybe we could have time now—'

Slowly, she nodded.

His expression lightened. 'I'm planning on visiting the Caribbean. Falcone isn't interested in any Viscari properties there, and I need to reassure my staff on that score. And I need to visit the site of the latest Viscari Hotel, on Ste Cecile.' He made a wry face. 'It was where I wanted to take you when I was so desperate to escape Rome!'

He shook his head, as if to shake the grim memory from him.

He looked straight at Eloise. 'Would you come there with me now?'

He saw rejection in her eyes—but saw conflict, too, and a flash of longing.

'Oh, Vito... I can't take any time off now—the Carldons need me.'

'Then may I come and visit you out on Long Island?'

Slowly she nodded. 'I... I usually have the weekends off, when the Carldons are home with Johnny.'

He smiled. His familiar warm, sweeping smile. 'This Saturday?'

Again, she nodded slowly. She could feel her heart-rate quicken, and made herself check the time.

'I have to go now,' she said. She looked across at him. 'Vito—it's...it's been good. Tonight—dinner... Just... just being with you. But I... I...well...please, I can't rush things... I...'

She fell silent, let her eyes drop. Emotion was thick in her throat.

This time yesterday I had no idea that tonight I would see him again. That all my feelings for him would be so different! That all my anger would be purged! That I'd be here with him, like this... Like I used to be...

But *was* it like it used to be? It couldn't be, could it? Not any more. Never again could there be just a casual romance between them. Now it could only be all...or nothing. And she did not know which. Not yet.

She felt the touch of his hand on hers, lightly brushing it with his fingers.

'It's whatever you want, Eloise,' he said. His voice was soft, intent. Sincere.

Her eyes lifted to his and for a moment, a long, long moment, their eyes simply met—acknowledging, accepting.

'Thank you,' she whispered, her voice low.

Then she drew back her hand, picked up her bag, got to her feet as he did likewise.

'I'll get the hotel limo to take you to your mother's apartment,' Vito said.

But Eloise shook her head. 'It's OK, I'll take a taxi. I'm used to New York now.' She smiled.

He walked her to the kerb as the doorman summoned one of the waiting cabs, then helped her in.

As she lowered herself into the seat he felt a rush of longing for her. How beautiful she was—how truly beautiful! From her golden hair to her long, long legs. Her slender waist and her full, ripe breasts, straining against the fabric of her top as she fastened her seat belt across her. Fuller and riper, surely, than he remembered...

He dragged his thoughts away. Made himself do nothing more than smile down at her as he closed the door, as she lifted a hand to wave him goodnight. The cab pulled off into the melee of Manhattan traffic. He watched it till it disappeared from sight.

Inside the cab, Eloise closed her eyes. Her head was in a whirl—and not just from the wine she was no longer used to. From something much, much headier.

Vito! Oh, Vito! My desire for you is as strong as ever! But I cannot just yield to it headlong!

Yet for all her self-admonition she felt the blood surge in her body, quickening her hectic pulse, heating her cheeks. Her eyes went to the window, to the traffic beyond, the neon lights and illuminated street signs, and they all blurred into a whirl of colour. Anguish filled her face. This time yesterday things had seemed so simple, the future so straightforward. Rigid, unforgiving—solitary. But now...

Now there was turmoil in her heart—turning her upside down, inside out, round and round and round.

A smothered cry came from her lips.

CHAPTER EIGHT

VITO PACED RESTLESSLY across his bedroom. He could not sleep. His mind was wide awake, replaying every single moment he had spent with Eloise that evening. Emotion jangled within him—one moment soaring, the next crashing, tangling itself into intractable knots within him. He'd tried to make sense of them, but it was hopeless.

He ran his hands through his hair, striding out into the lounge of his suite, stopping by the windows, staring out over the street below, and beyond that to the darkened mass of Central Park. As if he could see across the city to where she was—he did not know where precisely—at her mother's apartment.

Is she sleepless too? Is she thinking of me as I think of her? Unable to think of anything else at all?

It was a hope he kept on feeling, darting through him, keeping his heart-rate high. Longing filled him. For her to be so close—and yet so far!

Was it just desire that made him feel so? He knew desire was there—how could he not? It had leapt, fully formed, the moment he had set eyes on her, both that afternoon and then again that evening, as she walked into the bar.

Will I ever not feel desire for her?

The question hung in his head, and as he gazed unseeing at the cityscape beyond, seeing only the image that blazed like a jewel in his mind, he knew the question was unnecessary. The answer was foregone.

I will desire her all my life...

Even as he acknowledged it he felt another, deeper emotion well up beneath. His longing for her was not mere desire.

It is for her—for her herself! Everything about her—

He hauled himself away, feeling his heart pounding, hectic and strong. He did not know what name to give what he felt—knew only that it was an emotion that was the most powerful he had ever felt.

Resolved into a single word. A single name.

Eloise.

'All set?' Laura Carldon smiled at Eloise.

Eloise nodded, but a hollow feeling was emptying her insides. Her nerves were jangling.

Laura Carldon's smile widened. 'Great—you have a fantastic day with your gorgeous, gorgeous guy today! And, like I said, John and I are going to start looking for a replacement for you, now that—'

Consternation filled Eloise's face, making her cut across urgently. 'No—please—it's not necessary! I mean—it's too soon—I don't know—I just don't know!'

Laura Carldon looked at her straight. 'Ellie, Vito Viscari is giving you time, but you know...' and now her voice became pointed and her gaze penetrating '...there is only one outcome possible. You *know* that, Ellie—you know you do.'

Eloise's face paled. She knew why her employer was saying that—but it wasn't as straightforward as she thought it was. It wasn't straightforward at all! How could it possibly be?

To her relief, Laura backed off. She'd gone into big sister mode when Eloise had got back from Manhattan and blurted out everything about Vito, and her employer had been far more sympathetic to her predicament than her mother had been.

Eloise could still hear her mother's blunt advice ringing in her ears.

'You must do what you want, Eloise—and take the consequences of your decision. Just as I did. But it's your decision, not mine. What is it you want to do?'

But that was just it, wasn't it? she thought now, wretchedly. What *did* she want? And what did Vito want?

And, most importantly of all, what will he want when—? No, don't go there. Not yet. Not yet by a long, long way.

The hollow feeling scoured her insides. No, straightforward was the last thing it was.

'I've got to *know*, Laura!' Her plea was heartfelt. 'I've got to know what *he* feels. I've got to know what *I* feel! What we feel about each other—about...about *everything*!'

'Well, that's exactly why you need to spend time with him,' Laura Carldon said encouragingly. 'To start finding that out! An afternoon with him here on Long Island is ideal! Show him the sights, hit the beach, go shopping in the boutiques—have a nice long, lazy lunch. Have *fun*!'

In the hours that followed, Eloise heard her employer's admonition echoing in her head. Vito had arrived and been welcomed by Laura—she was casually dressed, but looking a carefully composed knock-out.

Laura's aside to Eloise of, 'OMG, he's *gorgeous*!' had been clearly audible.

And then Johnny had rushed out even more enthusiastically to greet the gleaming Ferrari Vito had rented while in the USA.

Eloise had climbed in and Vito had headed down the driveway, waving back at Johnny, hoisted up in his mother's arms, who had waved back mightily, mouthing, *Vroom! Vroom!* ecstatically.

Only as they turned out on to the roadway beyond the Carldons' extensive grounds did Eloise look at Vito in the confines of the car, punishingly aware of his presence so, so close to her. She felt her heart catch.

He was focusing on the road, and it gave her a precious moment to take in his gorgeousness—the feathered dark hair, the dark glasses, the chiselled profile, the way his cotton knit polo shirt moulded his leanly muscled torso, the glint of his gold watch at his wrist, the long length of his tanned bare forearm...

She gulped inwardly. The impact he had on her senses was as powerful—as overpowering!—as it had ever been. And by the same token she knew—had known from that first appreciative glance at her as he'd arrived—that he, too, was finding her just as appealing.

Thanks to her employer's insistence, she was looking just the part for a day out on fashionable Long Island—courtesy of Laura's own wardrobe.

'I'm keeping all this for next time around, but this will fit you perfectly now!' Laura had said, pulling out of her vast closet a pair of navy blue elastic-waisted trousers and a carefully constructed but very smart blue and white boat-necked, loose-fitting striped top, both with an extremely upmarket specialist fashion label. A pair of low-heeled white sandals and a straw shoulder bag completed her outfit.

With her hair pushed back off her forehead with a white headband, snaking down her back in a long plait, she looked, Eloise knew, both stylish and slim. And the appreciative glint in Vito's eyes confirmed it—sweeping her instantly back to a thousand memories of his eyes lighting upon her as she walked up to him in any number of his hotels across Europe. He'd only ever had eyes for her.

As if he'd read her mind, he glanced at her now as he drove, and even with the covering of his dark glasses she felt the force of his gaze.

'So, where shall we go?' he asked. There was a smile in his voice…around his mouth.

'The south coast is the most popular, and has the best beaches, but the north coast is less crowded and more historic,' she said.

'Well, I've never been to Long Island at all,' Vito said, relaxing his shoulders into the car seat that moulded his body, 'so it will all be great.'

He forbore to say that crossing a desert would be 'great' if he could do it with Eloise.

Eloise!

Her name billowed in his head, catching at his throat as his eyes drank her in, and he revelled in her presence at his side after the long, long months of being apart from her.

Did I really once take it for granted that I could spend any amount of time with her that I wanted—that she would always be there for me?

The thought was troubling. Its resolution less so. Never again, he knew with absolute certainty, would he ever take her for granted.

Did I win her too easily? Woo her too effortlessly? Did I assume she would wait to hear me out about the trap that Marlene had sprung on me—assume she would wait until I'd extricated myself from it?

Well, there would be no more assumptions about Eloise. He felt his pulse kick. She had the same impact on him now as she had had the very first time he'd set eyes on her, as she'd gazed up at him with her huge, beautiful blue eyes. He knew only that it was essential that he get this right. That they discover, once and for all, what they might be together. The most important question of all.

'OK,' he said, and deliberately he made his voice light and cheerful, 'tell me everything you know about Long Island!'

Eloise was glad of the lead. Glad that they could just chat, in a friendly, unforced way, about somewhere that—just for a change, she realised—she knew more about than he did. Previously, while they'd been touring Europe, most of the cities they'd gone to she had never been to before. It had been Vito who'd been knowledgeable about them. It was curious to think that this time around it would be *her* telling *him.*

Perhaps it was more than curious—perhaps it was symbolic? Symbolic of the subtle but undeniable change in their relationship. She was no longer the compliant girlfriend, endlessly willing to be anything he wanted. For the first time she felt more... More *what*, precisely?

More equal. More... I don't know... More grown up? Less...reliant?

It was something to ponder. But maybe not right now. When she had time—time to think, to feel, to try and know her own mind. Her own heart.

She gave a little shake of her head. For now, like Vito, she wanted only to keep the day easy. Enjoyable. 'Fun,' Laura had said. Well, that was good advice.

'OK,' she began, 'so, originally Long Island was home to several Native American peoples. Then, as they were moved off by the incoming Europeans, it was settled as farmland, both by the Dutch and the English, and then in the nineteenth century the railroads expanded, bringing yet more settlers, especially at the New York City

end—Brooklyn and so on. But by the end of the century
the very wealthy New Yorkers were heading up here to
build their massive mansions.'

She moved casually into a description of what she'd
learnt about Long Island since arriving at the Carldons' to
be Johnny's nanny. It seemed to work, and as she chatted,
interrupted by questions from Vito, she could feel herself starting to lose the acute self-consciousness she'd had
since they'd driven off. Unconsciously, it all became…
familiar.

Easy.

Natural.

By the time they stopped for lunch, in one of the attractive and extremely well-heeled resort villages of
the east end of the Hamptons, she felt for the first time
that maybe—just maybe—Laura Carldon's instruction
to 'have fun' might be just what she was doing. It was
good to be with Vito again! His sense of humour was
so attuned to hers, and the smiling glances he threw
her way, the observations he made—all just seemed to
come naturally.

As if we'd never been apart.

It was a strange, beguiling thought. And yet she knew,
with a sobering reminder, that it could never be as it had
once been.

But what could it yet be?

That was the question that haunted her. Yet even as
she thought it she felt resistance. Sitting here in the late
summer's heat, beneath the striped awning of the sho-
reside restaurant, watching the sun sparkle off the azure
sea, the array of expensive yachts bobbing in the harbour, how *could* she be haunted by it? How could she do
anything except what she was doing—enjoying being
with Vito.

The answer to my question will come, and what will be, will be.

That was all she knew for certain. All she could know for now.

Vito leaned back in his chair, replete after an extremely good lunch of freshly caught fish, washed down with a cold beer. A light breeze lifted the heat, as did the shade of the awning. Across the table, sipping at iced tea, Eloise was regaling him with tales of the Vanderbilts and the Morgans, and all those other mega-rich Americans from the Gilded Age who'd built their huge baronial mansions on the Gold Coast North Shore.

'I believe some of the mansions are open to the public,' she was saying. 'They're really the closest the Americans come to having stately homes! In fact,' she went on, 'I think quite a lot of the mansions were decorated with the contents of French *châteaux* and Scottish castles that were shipped over here in the nineteenth century. Fireplaces, mirrors, panelling—that sort of thing.'

Vito made a face. 'Well, I suppose we Europeans should take that as a compliment! Raiding our history to create theirs!' he said lightly. His expression changed. 'Do you remember our visit to Versailles, that very first time in Paris? You wanted to see the Trianon palaces as well—both the Grand and the Petit—so we did the whole lot in one day!'

Eloise smiled. 'You were very forbearing,' she said.

'I wanted to please you,' he replied.

Her gaze flickered. *Had* Vito wanted to please her? Had he made an effort for her? Not just on that day, but throughout their time together? Did his air of charm and ease camouflage the amount of effort he'd put into their relationship?

Her mother's view was that it had been she who'd done

all the pleasing, who had gone along with whatever Vito had wanted. Maybe, though, that wasn't fair.

Just because I didn't notice it, it doesn't mean he wasn't doing it...

A little glow formed inside her, and her smile at him was warm. 'It was a wonderful day!' she said. 'I shall always treasure it!'

His dark velvet eyes softened. 'We had good times, didn't we?' he said.

She took another sip of her iced tea. 'Yes, we had good times,' she echoed. Her expression changed, becoming troubled. 'Is that what we're trying to do now, Vito? Recapture the past? Make today…and the next time you visit…like the times we had together?'

Eloise's eyes slid away, out over the sparkling blue water of the quayside. From here, Europe seemed so very far away. So very long, long ago.

Her eyes shadowed. 'We can't go back, Vito,' she said, her gaze returning to him.

She saw him give a quick, decisive shake of his head. 'I don't want to go back,' he said.

He paused, and she felt his eyes suddenly reaching deep inside her—felt it like a jolt of electricity passing through her innermost being. She felt emotion flex around it like a strong magnetic field, engendered by him.

He spoke again, his words clear. 'I want to go forward, Eloise. Into the future.'

She heard him speak, felt the slug of her heart, felt his gaze holding hers. She saw him lift his hand, gesture all around him.

'A future for the two of us.'

His eyes were fixed on hers. He could not take them from her. In his head his own words echoed—*'the two of us.'* That was what he wanted. A future with Eloise. Only Eloise. He knew that—felt it all the way through him with a certainty that was flowing through him now as if a sluice gate had opened. It was as ineluctable as the tide flowing in from the depths of the ocean, lapping at the shore.

He felt all his emotions—so turbulent, so torn—finally resolved, after so much confusion. *This* was what he wanted—he knew that now, knew it with a certainty that he could not deny or question. It was all coming together now, in this moment.

Emotion flowed with the tide of certainty in a powerful sweeping through his consciousness. He did not need more time, more wondering, more questioning. It was not necessary. He knew—he *knew*. Knew everything he needed to know about Eloise—about his feelings for her. More than desire, more than passion.

There is nothing she can say or do that will change that. I want my future—my whole future—to be with her. To be with Eloise.

It was a name he had said so often, and it had meant what he had not yet known—but now he did.

Eloise.

The woman he wanted—the *only* woman he wanted. The only woman he would *ever* want in his life.

I wondered if it was her—wondered if she could be for me, if we were destined to be together all our lives. And now I know. She is—she is that one.

The certainty of it seared through him. His hand dropped, seeking hers to turn it over in his, to mesh his fingers with hers—mesh his life with hers.

For a moment—so brief—he felt her hand tremble beneath his. And then she slipped it away, out of his grasp. The expression in her eyes changed.

'Do you mean that?'

Her voice was little more than a whisper, and the expression in her eyes was one he could not read—as if a fine veil had fallen across them, dimming them.

He took a breath. 'Yes—beyond anything. Beyond everything.'

He spoke in a low voice, but there was certainty in it, a clarity she could not misunderstand. He paused, holding that veiled expression in her eyes, feeling in his chest the thump of his heart, as if giving emphasis to every word he said.

'You may say this is too soon—too fast. But for me it is not. For me, Eloise, it has been in the making ever since you left me.' His eyes worked, showing a flash of pain. 'When you left—it hurt, Eloise. But I could not allow myself to give in to the pain—I had to continue with the bitter farce of my engagement to Carla. But the pain was there all the time, deep within me.'

He paused again.

'It was that pain that made me turn away from her on our wedding day—that gave me the determination to show that this was something I could not—*should* not— go through with. And that pain...' He took a breath, ragged now. 'That pain stayed with me all the while I searched for you—and it stabbed me yet again, deeper and more dreadfully, when, after I'd finally found you, you told me—again—to get out of your life.'

He paused once more, his eyes searching hers now, trying to pierce that fine veil that still masked them.

'There is only one time I do not feel that pain, Eloise. It's when I'm with you—'

He reached for her hand again, hardly aware that he was doing so, knowing only that it was a need within him he had to obey. And this time she did not withdraw from him. This time she let his fingers mesh with hers, fasten around hers. Warming his.

'And there is only one reason for that, Eloise—there

can *be* only one. Because you've become my life—the reason for it.' His hand gripped hers, his voice urgent. 'Eloise, make your future with me—make our future together.'

'Do you mean that? Do you truly mean it, Vito?'

It was the same question, the same doubt, the same low, strained tone of voice. The same searching of her eyes.

'With all my heart,' he said. 'We are so good together— we are so *right*! It's always been like that, Eloise—*always*! From the very start.'

Her expression changed. 'I was just one more leggy blonde in your life...' she said.

Vito shook his head, his thumb caressing the surface of her hand. 'Oh, no—so much, much more.' His voice was as caressing as his touch. 'Eloise, I *knew* there was something different about you—everything with you was so...so *natural*. So *right*.'

He took a breath, knowing what he had to say now.

'Eloise, believe me—please, please believe me—if you felt I ever took you for granted it was not so, not in the way you fear! Yes, romance has always come easy to me—I admit it, confess it. But you...you were always different. It was that sense of...of *rightness* between us. How we were together. It was that I took for granted, not you!' His voice changed, becoming darker, with a thread of pain in it. 'Losing you has shown me that all I want...all I crave...is to make my future with you. My precious Eloise.'

His eyes were soft as he said her name, as soft as velvet, and she felt their power over her senses...and her sense.

'It's too soon,' she faltered.

But her blood was surging in her body, quickening her pulse, heating her beyond the external heat of Long Island in the summer.

'But you're not saying no?' Vito's reply was quick, his eyes still holding hers.

Heat fanned out across her cheeks. Emotion was powerful within her. Impelling her onwards. Sweeping her forward on a tide, carrying her out of the safe harbour where she had taken shelter after the storm of Vito's betrayal.

But—whatever answer she might want to give—she had to hold back. She must not let herself be swept away—not again. Not now, when it was not just about herself. Or him.

Her eyes dipped. 'You said no pressure—' She could hardly get the words out.

Instantly she felt him acknowledge what she'd said. His hold on her hand slackened, relinquished her. He nodded, his mouth set, but resolute for all that.

'And I will abide by that. You have my word.' Briefly, he touched her knuckle with his forefinger. 'I have told you what I feel. I will not change, Eloise. I am here for you...for your future...if you will have me. Always. Whatever life brings us, I will be here for you.'

He took another breath and then, as if with a deliberate act of will, he reached for his beer, taking a last mouthful to finish it. She watched him—watched the strong muscles of his neck as he swallowed, watched the curve of his fingers around the glass. Heard the echo of his words inside her.

'Whatever life brings us...'

If that were true...

She felt emotion flare within her. Emotion that she dared not give a name to. Not yet...

He set down the glass, smiled across at her. An open smile, an easy smile. As if the intensity of their discourse had not happened at all.

'So,' he said, 'where shall we go after lunch?'

Relief filled her—and something more. Something that hovered over the rest of the afternoon like an aura around her, a golden haze that she wanted to immerse herself in. But it was a temptation she dared not indulge in.

Not yet... Not yet...

The most important question of all—the one she *had* to discover the answer to—still awaited. And everything would depend on the answer.

CHAPTER NINE

THE RENTED FERRARI crunched slowly along the gravel as Vito swung it up to the front door of the Carldons' house, turning off the engine. Silence lapped around them. He turned to Eloise. He was smiling, but she could see in his eyes a tension, a question.

For the rest of the day, as they'd taken their ease, exploring the far reaches of the island like tourists, they had kept things simple, light-hearted. Fun. Unpressured. But now, at the moment of their imminent parting, she could feel that pressure mount again.

'Will you think of what I've said to you?' Vito asked, his voice low, his eyes expressive.

Eloise's gaze flickered. 'How could I not?' she countered.

He nodded. 'For now, that is all I ask,' he said. Then his expression changed. 'I must fly down to Ste Cecile tomorrow,' he said. 'I can't postpone it any longer.'

'Of course,' Eloise said. Her gaze flickered again. 'Will...will you be coming back to New York afterwards, or going straight back to Rome?'

His answer was another question. 'Would you rather I went straight to Rome?' he asked.

His eyes rested on her, but she could see there was a veil over them. Her hand twisted on the handle of Laura Carldon's straw bag. She could feel her heart beating.

'I... I think you should come back to New York,' she

said. Her voice was low, as if she found speaking difficult. She made herself look at him straight. 'Because you asked me at lunch if…if I…' She swallowed. 'But then, you might change your mind when you're in the Caribbean.'

His voice cut right across her. 'No—I will not be changing my mind, Eloise! I meant what I said—I meant it with all my being! And nothing can change that—nothing!'

There was no veil in his eyes now, no hesitation in his voice. Only certainty.

He took her hand. 'I want no dissension between us ever again. I will never try to hide anything from you again, as I did in Rome. Nor will I hide my feelings for you.'

She felt colour flush along her cheekbones, saw long lashes dip over his dark eyes. She held completely still as his head lowered to hers and his mouth brushed softly on her lips, which quivered beneath his brief, caressing touch—a touch she had not felt for so, so long… As he drew back again his eyes held hers, as they had done so often before.

'Vito, I—'

Her voice was a breath, her eyes aglow—yet in his face was a wariness she knew she must not, dared not ignore. But what she was going to say?

The noise of the front door being tugged open made her start, and a small powerhouse of energy barrelled out on to the wide carriage sweep, closely followed by Laura Carldon.

With a resigned grin Vito opened his door, and a gleeful Johnny clambered in and settled himself on his lap, grabbing the steering wheel with enthusiastic cries of 'Vroom, vroom!'

Laura Carldon leaned on the open door. Eloise saw

that she was still looking a total knock-out, even though she'd simply spent the day at home.

'I couldn't hold him back any longer!' Laura laughed. She held out her hand to her son. 'Come on, Mr Trouble, out you get!'

Her son ignored her. 'Make it go!' he ordered Vito. Then, belatedly, he added, 'Please! Please! *Please!*'

Vito cast a look at Eloise's employer. 'Are you OK if I just drive down to the gate with him and back? I'll be very careful.'

'Yes! Yes! *Yes!*' shouted Johnny, adding another, 'Vroom! Vroom!' for good measure.

Laura smiled. 'You're a very lucky young man,' she informed her son, and she stood back and closed the car door for Vito.

'Sit quietly, Johnny,' Eloise instructed, 'or Vito can't start the engine.'

Good as gold, Johnny settled on Vito's lap, his hands still on the steering wheel. Vito started the engine and pressed the accelerator to let the engine give its characteristic throaty roar, then lessened it to start the car moving very slowly, his hands resting lightly over Johnny's, giving the little boy the sensation that he was steering. Johnny chortled happily to himself, clearly in his element.

Eloise watched them—the little boy sitting on Vito's lap, and Vito quite at ease with him, advising him to steere right as they veered left, and talking to him about the car. Her expression was strange...her gaze intent as she watched him interact with the little boy.

The expedition did not take long. Soon they were circling back to the front door again, and Vito let Johnny sound the horn in a satisfyingly loud manner before lifting him out of the car and handing him to his waiting mother. He climbed out himself, gracefully, opening the passenger door for Eloise to emerge.

Laura cast a grateful glance at Vito. 'Thank you! As you can see, Johnny's just a tad obsessed with cars!'

'Vroom! Vroom!' confirmed Johnny happily, and ran around driving an imaginary car.

Vito grinned indulgently. 'I think the English term is "petrol head",' he said.

Laura caught her perambulating son. 'Now, what do you say to Signor Viscari, young man?'

'Thank you, thank you, *thank you*!' Johnny said in a rush.

Vito ruffled his hair. 'You're welcome,' he said.

He glanced at Eloise. She was standing very still, just watching him. Her expression was very strange. As if she were both a million miles away and simultaneously totally focused on him. Absently, he wondered at it, then turned his attention to her employer.

'He's a great kid,' he said, and grinned, nodding at Johnny.

Laura beamed—both at his praise for her beloved young son and at being the recipient of Vito's mega-voltage smile. 'And you're great with him,' she responded. 'A natural. But then...' She smiled at him, but her eyes, Vito could not fail to see, had darted to Eloise, who still had that strange fixated look on her face. 'Italian men are famed for being great with children.'

There was a minute pause—so brief Vito wondered if he'd actually noticed it.

Then Laura went on, with distinct self-consciousness, 'You'll be a natural when it comes to your own!'

Her voice was light, but once again he was sure she glanced between her lashes at her son's nanny.

Then her gaze went back to him. 'Will you come in for drinks? My husband will be home soon from the golf course.'

He shook his head, made his voice regretful. 'Thank

you, but I'd better not. I'm flying down to the Caribbean tomorrow, to check on my latest build there, on Ste Cecile, and I must spend this evening touching base with my affairs back in Europe.'

Laura's face fell—but not, Vito felt, because he'd refused her offer.

'But you'll be coming back to New York?' she said quickly.

He saw her throw another swift look at Eloise, who was still standing quietly, her expression unreadable.

'Most certainly,' he assured her, his smile warm.

Laura's face relaxed. 'Great,' she said. 'And then you really must come over for dinner—or maybe brunch at the weekend.' She looked down at her son, who was tugging on her hand. 'Just wait a moment, Johnny...' she began.

Eloise was there instantly, galvanised into action. 'I'll take him,' she said, conscious that she *was*, after all, the nanny.

She turned to Vito.

'I hope you have a good trip tomorrow, and that everything is...is OK at the site, and with—well, everything,' she said, feeling awkward. Feeling a whole lot more than awkward.

'Thank you,' he said. 'I'm sure it will be. The build is all on schedule, and we're still on track to open as planned next month. Maybe,' he said, and now it was as if his eyes were speaking, 'you'll be able to take some holiday time round about then.'

'Definitely!' Laura's voice was enthusiastic. 'We'll make sure she's free.'

Vito smiled at her. 'Thank you,' he said.

It was what he needed to hear—he needed to know that Eloise would be free to come with him, to be with him.

If she wanted to.

*But does she? Will she? Is what I said to her what she
wanted to hear?*

His eyes went to her now. She was hunkered down by
Johnny, asking him about his day with his mother and
Maria. Then her employer took her son's hand, talking
straight to Eloise.

'Ellie, I'll take Johnny indoors—you say goodbye to
Vito. No need to rush.'

Laura lifted a hand in farewell to Vito, with a final
admonition for him to come over next weekend, and
wished him a good flight south. Then she swept inside
with Johnny.

Vito's eyes went back to Eloise, who'd straightened.
She was clutching her straw bag tightly on her shoulder. He went up to her and took her hands, holding them
lightly, his eyes only for her.

'Thank you for today,' he said softly. 'It has meant
so much to me.' He took a breath. 'Think, I beg you, on
what I have said. I mean every word, Eloise. I could not
be more sure of them,' he said.

The grip on her hands tightened momentarily, and his
voice deepened.

'I want you to be my future, Eloise—to be with me always, to make your life with mine. I have no doubts, no
questions, about that. What happened between us—that
nightmare in Rome—has only served to make me absolutely sure of that. *Absolutely* sure. You mean everything
to me—and you always will.'

He gave a smile—a brief, flickering smile. 'Take all
the time you need before giving me your answer. If it is
when I return to New York—or even if it's later, or next
year, or at any time—I will be ready for it.'

For one last, endless moment his eyes held hers and
she felt their force, their power reaching into her, trans-

forming her. She felt again that shimmer of joy she had felt in the car, before little Johnny had erupted upon them.

Her expression changed. *He'd been so good with him.* Laura Carldon's description echoed in her head. 'A natural', she'd called him.

She felt her throat tighten suddenly. Then Vito was lifting her hands to his mouth, one after another, kissing each softly. She felt joy, deep emotion, felt a golden glow encircling her—transforming her.

'Oh, Vito!' Her voice caught, and then it was her hands that were tightening on his before, with a reluctance she could not hide, she drew them from him, stepped away.

Emotion filled her, overflowed as she watched him get back into the car, lower the window to crook his elbow across it as he turned on the ignition. His eyes were on her—warm, soft, filled with emotion.

'My Eloise,' he said, and in his voice was all the emotion that was in his eyes.

Then, with a wave of his hand, he engaged the engine and the car moved away, crunching down the drive to disappear through the open gates on to the road beyond.

She went on watching until she could hear it no more.

But inside her head she heard still the echo of his last words to her.

'My Eloise.'

To her relief, Laura Carldon did not grill her about Vito. Eloise needed mental privacy to let the turmoil inside her find its resolution, and though she went through the motions of looking after her charge she knew her mind was not really on Johnny.

With the Carldons in their Manhattan apartment midweek, there was only Maria, her beaming manner indicating that she was taking it for granted that Vito had flown the Atlantic to claim Eloise as his own.

Yet Eloise knew it could not be that simple. She must not rush, nor make assumptions—must not, above all, be carried away with all the emotion swelling in her breast, hearing only that yearning echo of his words to her.

'My Eloise.'

Because it was not just about her—not just about the two of them. It could not be. It was about much, much more. Into her head came the image of her mother—falling so head over heels in love with her father. A love that had proved so disastrous in the end. And not just for her mother.

I can't make the mistake she did.

Far too much was at stake for that.

I have to be sure.

Restlessly, unable to sleep for all the thoughts and emotions circling endlessly in her head, she paced her bedroom, feeling the import of the decision she *had* to make. Not just the one she *wanted* to make...

Over the baby monitor she heard Johnny stir in his sleep. She smiled faintly as she thought she heard a murmured 'Vroom, vroom...' as he dreamt, doubtless of fast cars. She heard, too, in her head, Laura Carldon's voice, praising Vito's manner with her beloved son.

She pressed a hand to her mouth, feeling emotion surging up inside her.

Surely I can be sure of him? Surely I can?

When he was back from the Caribbean—when he came to see her again—she must delay no longer. She would put her future in his hands. Tell him everything. Everything that was in her heart and more—oh, so much more...

And with all my heart I hope he'll feel the joy that I do.

Her employer, having returned to Long Island on Thursday, made it very plain that she had no doubt that Eloise was making the right decision. The *only* decision, to her mind.

'You and Vito can have the run of the place till Sunday,' she said meaningfully.

Eloise's gaze veered away, her colour heightening.

'John and I are away Saturday night with friends, and Maria and Giuseppe will be at their daughter's that evening too. So you can have fun here, you and Vito, with young Johnny.'

Her expression changed. Took on that pointed look it had had when Vito had dropped her off.

'Ellie, you can see from the way he is with Johnny that Vito's going to be a *great* family guy—he is *definitely* marriage material, not just good for a tempestuous romance. He's a *keeper*, honey. So keep him!'

She swept off, not giving Eloise a chance to reply, leaving her words to echo in her head. A little knot formed in her stomach. Tomorrow—whatever came of it—she would know how her life would be. Her whole life.

She felt the knot tighten.

It stayed tight right up until the moment when Vito's Ferrari swept up the drive, shortly before lunchtime on Saturday. Johnny excitedly rushed her downstairs, where Vito was greeting Giuseppe warmly in their native Italian, handing him a bottle of champagne to chill. Her charge was pleading for another ride in the Ferrari.

Vito stooped down, ruffling Johnny's hair with an easy gesture. 'Definitely,' he promised him. 'But not right now, OK?'

Then he straightened and looked up towards the head of the staircase, where Eloise was poised.

His eyes blazed as they lit on her, and she felt their force. Reeled from it. Her hand tightened on the banister as if to steady herself. For steady she must be. This was not the time to rush down the stairs and into his arms...

In her mind's eye she was back as she had been the day Vito had first found her in Long Island, her heart thumping, pulse pounding with disbelief that he was really there, in the flesh, after all those anguished months since she'd fled Rome. How she'd stood paralysed and trembling, emotions knifing her from all directions.

How different it is now from then.

'Eloise...'

Vito's soft utterance of her name summoned her, and he stood gazing up at her as she started to head down towards him. She'd dressed with care that morning, not wearing one of her usual casual outfits she adopted when on nanny duty. Today—consciously—she wore a warm vermilion sun dress, smocked over her bust, with shoe-string straps and a floaty calf-length skirt.

It had passed muster with Laura, who'd checked her out before she'd set off with her husband earlier.

'Ideal,' she'd said. 'And wear your hair down—at least until you go swimming.'

Eloise's expression had tautened. 'I can't swim! Not until—'

'Exactly,' Laura had responded, and there had been another meaningful look in her eye. Then she'd nodded. 'I want it all sorted, Ellie, by the time we get home tomorrow—understood?' she'd said, clearly in big sister mode. 'And I expect your engagement ring diamond to be the size of the Ritz, OK? Though maybe that's the wrong hotel, in the circumstances!'

She'd laughed, and swept off.

Now, as she made her graceful descent to the hall below, Eloise could feel the loosely gathered folds of her dress floating around her bare legs, her long hair falling like a waterfall down her back. Her make-up was subtle, but emphasised the blue of her eyes and the golden tan she'd acquired during the summer, and she knew, with absolute certainty, that the glow in Vito's dark, lambent eyes was for her and her alone.

And it always will be.

She felt joy lift inside her and a smile part her lips. She saw his eyes warm, and he stepped forward towards her. He took her hand and kissed it, murmuring to her. Behind him Giuseppe hovered shamelessly—ready, as Eloise was well aware, to report back as required to his wife Maria.

The lover come to claim his beloved—and have their happy-ever-after ending...

She felt that little lift of emotion again—and then behind it a downward drag, as if of deep water pulling at her. In her ears rang Laura's admonition, and she felt a longing inside her...a longing to tell Vito all she yearned to tell him.

But the timing must be right—perfect... Later—when we are alone...

Certainly not right now. Right now it was time to respond to Vito's arrival, and to listen to Giuseppe saying that he would serve lunch out at the pool house in half an hour. This gave Johnny an opening to demand that Vito come up and see all *his* cars—namely the extensive collection of toy vehicles that adorned his day nursery.

So the three of them duly went back upstairs, where Johnny and Vito got stuck into some intensive playtime. Eloise sat back, watching Vito sprawled on the carpet with her charge, entering into the childish spirit of racing toy cars—with appropriate vocal soundtrack. She felt a huge upwelling of emotion ballooning inside her.

'He's going to be a great family guy.'

Again, she could hear Laura's words in her head. And she knew them to be true. So, so true. Which meant...

The house phone went and she picked it up, then turned to Vito and Johnny. 'That's lunch,' she said.

They headed down to the pool, set amongst the spacious lawns of the Carldons' mansion, complete with its own pool house opposite.

Under the shaded terrace Maria and Giuseppe were setting out a lavish *al fresco* lunch. Maria, beaming from ear to ear, fussed over them as they took their places, chattering away to Vito in too-rapid Italian. Her eyes were only for him as his wickedly attractive smile brought the colour to her plump cheeks.

And to Eloise's as well—she could feel her stomach clench with raw, quickening desire.

Then Johnny's needs diverted her, and she had to pay attention to him, helping him to cold roast chicken and salad, letting him pour—carefully—juice from the iced jug at his place.

As she did so Maria and Giuseppe departed, and Vito hefted the opened champagne bottle from its ice bucket, gently pouring out generous measures for them both. He set hers before her, and lifted his glass to her.

'To us,' he said, and let his gaze rest on her.

The simple toast dared her to refute it—but she did not, and he felt his spirits soar.

Yes—she will say yes to me! I know she will. It is in everything about her—her whole attitude towards me, her eyes upon me, her smiling at me... It can mean only one answer for me. Yes—yes and yes!

He looked at her over his glass, watched her take a sip from hers, let his eyes mingle with hers, let the openness in her gaze let him in, welcome him. Warmth filled him—and a joy he had not felt before in all his life. How perfect everything was—how absolutely perfect!

Eloise—my Eloise!

Then a little voice was piping up indignantly. 'To me too!' Johnny said, lifting up his beaker with both hands.

Vito duly tilted his glass to him. '*Saluti!* To you as well, young Gianni! That's Italian for Johnny.'

'That's what Maria calls me!' Johnny exclaimed, pleased, and drank a hefty slug of juice.

Lunch passed convivially, with Johnny clearly in his element having both of them paying him attention. But for all the child-centred conversation Eloise knew that another conversation was taking place too—between her and Vito. A conversation that was leading towards only one answer. An answer that she would give later, when the time was right. Perfect.

But before that, inevitably, came a session of pool play.

Watching Vito strip down to his swim shorts, exposing his lean, sculpted torso, his long, powerful thighs, brought back that flush of colour, the raw rush of desire, of burning memory, to Eloise. Even as he disported himself with a gleeful Johnny in the water, with huge amounts of splashing and chasing, in a game involving a myriad of inflatable pool toys, Eloise could not take her eyes from him.

She'd used the excuse of being too full and too lazy to do anything but relax in a shady lounger, sipping at the last of her allotted glass of champagne, and it afforded her the wondrous opportunity to feast her eyes on Vito.

Vito, Vito, Vito!

Oh, how the memories rushed back—themselves in Europe, day after day, night after night! Yes, it had been a dream of a romance then—but now... Oh, now it was so, *so* much more!

Yet again, Laura Carldon's words sounded in her head. *'He's a keeper, honey, so keep him!'*

And she would—she *would* keep him. Keep Vito close by her side, in her heart, all her life...*all* her life...

Surely what she desired so much would be! Surely all her fears were groundless, baseless! Surely Vito would sweep her into his arms with joy.

Emotion welled up in her, filling her, bringing joy and wonder to her whole being.

'I'm thirsty!'

Johnny's piping voice from the pool roused her from her reverie.

Effortlessly hefting the little boy up to the deck, Vito followed suit himself, and both of them came up to her. Eloise handed Johnny a beaker of chilled diluted juice, which he gulped down noisily, while Eloise wrapped him in a towel, sitting him down beside her on the lounger to pat him dry.

He handed back the beaker and gave a huge yawn.

'Time for your afternoon nap,' she announced.

It was Vito who carried him up to his nursery in the main house, then settled him on his bed with a light throw over him. As he fell asleep Maria's head came round the door. She announced that she would sit with him, and ushered Vito and Eloise firmly out of the nursery.

As they headed downstairs Eloise felt Vito's fingers slide between hers, catching her hand. The gesture felt so right, so natural. Her heart gave that little lift again.

Out by the pool house Maria had cleared away the remains of lunch, replacing them with a tray of freshly made fragrant coffee, and Eloise poured them both a cup. Vito sat himself down not on a lounger but on the padded swing seat, patting the place beside him. She took it without hesitation—but with a quickening of her pulse. Her eyes fluttered to his, then back to her coffee cup, and studiedly she sipped at the contents, burningly conscious of Vito at her side. So close—so close now...

As she bent her head slightly to drink she felt the soft brush of his hand down her back, smoothing the long fall of her hair. It sent a million shimmers through her.

She set down the coffee on the low table beside the seat, aware that Vito was doing the same on his side.

'Eloise...' The husk in his voice was audible in the sensual murmur of her name.

She turned to him—and reeled. The blaze in his eyes was open now, filling his dark, dark eyes, turning them to liquid fire. Desire was blatant in them. He did not speak, nor did she, as his other hand lifted to her. The tips of his fingers grazed the delicate outline of her jaw with a feathering lightness that sent those shimmers reverberating through her again. With infinite slowness, infinite gentleness, the tip of his finger shaped her mouth, and at her back she felt his hand press into the hollow of her spine, starting to draw her to him.

She should speak—halt him—should say to him what she must say...what she had been waiting to say, what she had waited so long to say but had dared not until she had known for absolute certain that to speak was right...

But his mouth was lowering to hers, her name was soft on his lips, and then his mouth was on hers, and her eyes were fluttering shut so she could take absolute focus on the bliss of the sensation of his mouth brushing hers— like water on a parched desert. Unconsciously her hand lifted to him, to glide around the strong column of his neck. She let her fingers splay into the silkiness of his hair, to mould the shape of his head to her palm as her other hand flattened against his muscled flank.

His mouth was opening hers, deepening their kiss, and she gave a little moan of pleasure in her throat. It seemed to shake him, so that he jerked her towards him, his hold on her strengthening.

'*Por Dio*, but I've missed you so much!'

His voice was thick as his mouth drew away fom hers momentarily, and she could hear the naked desire in his voice, bringing back a hundred memories—a thousand— of all their nights of passion. She felt faint, her blood rushing in her veins, sending heat to her core, and she could feel her breasts swelling, their peaks cresting. How long since she had felt like this in Vito's heady embrace? Too long—oh, too, *too* long.

Her breathing quickened, and with a hunger that his touch had released in her she pulled his mouth down to hers again wordlessly, knowing only that she wanted him, craved him, needed him now—*right* now.

He answered her need, crushing her mouth with his, sending a million nerve fibres into overdrive, catching at her lips with his, with skilled expertise, with mastery and possession. And she was his—oh, she was his—and he was hers, hers, *hers*.

For ever now—for ever he is mine!

The words soared in her mind, exultant. The world had gone—disappeared—the air and the sun had gone too. There was only Vito and herself. Only her body, quickening to his, aching for his possession as he had possessed it so many times before. She felt the muscles in her legs strain as she yearned towards him, wanting with a primal urgency to feel her swollen breasts crushed against him, to press her body against his.

Her need for him was answered, and he groaned, devouring her mouth yet more deeply. His hand left her face, stroked sensually down the column of her neck, palmed the rich swell of her breast, and she moaned with pleasure. His thumb caught at its crested peak and she moaned again, straining towards him. Then his hand was gliding still lower, down over her flank, cupping her hip.

Her thighs loosened and the heat in her core was melting her now, as she felt the rush of her own arousal. And then his hand was shaping that vee, pressing into it through the flimsy material of her sun dress with exquisite sensation as her hunger for him climbed and climbed. His long fingers splayed upwards, curving around the swell of her abdomen.

And then he froze.

Time stopped. Halted.

In a fraction of a second—less—he had pulled away from her, was staring at her with disbelief in his face. The material of her sundress was pulled taut against the curve of her body, outlining with absolute delineation those revealing contours.

Words in Italian broke from him. Disjointed. Shocked. Disbelieving.

As if pulled out of the drowning tide of physical desire, Eloise realised what he was seeing. What all the carefully chosen outfits she'd worn in his company had been designed to conceal. What now could be concealed no longer.

He jack-knifed to his feet, still staring down at her, horror-struck.

It was that horror-struck expression that penetrated her thoughts like some huge, heavy battering ram, shattering the crystalline delusions of her hopes. And then, even as it did so, his expression changed. Closed.

He took a step back.

'Is it mine?'

The cruelty of the words was like a knife. Slashing through what she had thought was between them. Had hoped, longed so much was between them.

But her fears had been right all along. That was the hideous, unbearable truth of it. The fears that had driven her from that moment in New York when she had discovered that her flight from Rome had *not* been the end of her affair with Vito. Could never be the end—because the consequences of it would be with her all her life.

All her child's life.

The child whose father was now staring at her with a look of horror on his face. Telling her what she had dreaded to know.

Rejection. Rejection just as my father rejected me.

The pain of it made her faint, but she must give an answer.

'I think you had better leave, Vito.' Her voice came from very far away.

'Do you carry my child?'

The vehemence in his voice was searing, and the burning in his gaze was upon her like a laser.

She looked at him, her expression twisting. There was a gaping hole inside her that was getting larger every second, swallowing her.

'Do you *really* think, Vito—' the words were gritted from her, each one heavier than a stone, harder than granite '—that I would have let you come near me again here in the USA if I had been carrying another man's child? Do you really think that?'

His expression changed. She could see it happening, see logic morphing through his eyes to create an entirely different expression. One that chilled her even more than his horror had chilled her.

'So when were you going to tell me?'

The question was tautly spoken, with a distant dispassion that made it sound almost remote. Yet there was nothing remote in the emotion that was surging through him now, leaping in his blood, his heart. Nothing remote in the voice that was crying out in his head.

She carries my child! My child—our child!

He felt faint with it...with the knowledge of it. With the wonder of it. But another emotion was slicing through him, freezing his face as she stumbled into her answer.

'Today. Later— I mean...' She swallowed, stumbling, stammering again, hardly knowing what she was saying so huge was the hole inside her, swallowing her. 'This afternoon. I was going to tell you while Johnny was hav-

ing his nap, but then you kissed me and...' Her voice
trailed off.

He did not reply, only went on looking at her. His face
was shuttered still, and it reminded her with a blow of
how he'd looked when she had come to him in the bar of
the hotel that was no longer his—that her mistrust of him
had caused him to lose, along with half of his inheritance.

Wary. He looked wary. As if she could do him irrepa-
rable damage. As if she already had.

Again.

She reached a hand towards him, but he stood too far
from her. 'Vito, I—'

There was urgency in her voice. Desperation. But he
would not hear it. Refused to hear it. Emotion was storming inside him, but he refused to hear that too. Refused everything except the harsh, harrowing question he wanted
to throw at her now. Even as he prepared to speak it he
knew it was not what he wanted to say. What he wanted
to do.

*Wrap your arms around her—sweep her to you. Hug
her closer than the child she carries so that you are inseparable from her, inseparable from your child.*

But his voice cut across all that.

'How could you not tell me the very moment you
knew? How could you keep it from me? *How?*' he demanded again.

Emotion stormed through him—and horror too.

'Dio mio,' he breathed as realisation hit him. 'I might
be married to Carla! Do you not see that? I could have
married another woman.'

Cold pooled in him. Had he not jilted Carla... The
horror of what he might have done, in total ignorance,
made him harsh.

'I could have married Carla and never known I had a
son, or a daughter! Were you *insane* to do such a thing?

To carry my child without my knowledge? To risk deny-
ing our child its father? How *dare* you do such a thing?'
Anger lashed from him at the enormity of what she'd
done. 'How *dare* you?'

The cold was pooling in him again, arctic in its horror.
Had he not found her again—had he not come to America—she would have borne his child—*their* child—without his knowledge. A child who would not know its own
father—who would be deprived of his love, his devotion.

Memory thrust into him of his own father, whom he
had loved so much, and to whom he had been the apple
of his eye, his beloved only child. There was memory and
there was grief—always that stab of grief that would always be there—for the loss of his father, taken before his
time. And now *he* might have been a father parted from
his child—parted by his total ignorance of its existence.

I would not have known I had a child to love!

His mother, so despairingly bereft since his father's untimely death, would never have known she had a grandchild.

Pain convulsed him at the thought of what had so
nearly been lost. A child bereft of its father, never to
know its doting grandmother, to be raised in an alien land
by a woman who thought it acceptable to deny a father
his child...to deny her child a father who would love his
child with all his heart and being.

'How *dared* you not tell me?' he hurled at her again.

His fury excoriated her, made her gasp with the force
of it. She had never felt it before—never known it. She
had always been the cherished one, the desired one, the
wooed one, the one Vito had sought only to win her back.
And now the tide of his fury was drowning her so that
she could not breathe, could not speak, could do nothing
but stand there, aghast, as it poured over her.

His was face was contorted as a harsh intake of breath ravaged his lungs. His mouth twisted as he spoke.

'We shall be married the moment it can be arranged. Our child will *not* be born out of wedlock. That is all that matters now. Nothing else.'

He saw her try to speak, but he would not let her. What could she say in her defence? *Nothing!* There was nothing she could say to justify her silence! Justify the risk she had run that he might marry another woman, lose his own child...

He plunged on, his voice knifing the air.

'All that matters is that you are pregnant with my child and that had I not found you, here in America, I would not have known about it.'

He looked at her, his eyes bleak.

'How could you do that, Eloise? *How?* Knowing all these months and never telling me! Keeping it from me? What kind of woman *does* that?'

He shook his head. A heaviness was crushing him. Crushing everything he'd hoped for, longed for. How could this be the woman he'd thought her to be? Longed for her to be?

He could not stay here—not now. He had to get away. The storm inside him was impossible to bear—impossible!

Her face was stark, as white as a sheet, and she was reaching towards him, imploring him with her very gesture.

But he held up his hands, backed away. 'I have to go,' he said, his voice staccato. 'I can't speak more now—'

He broke off, throat convulsing. He could not take this in—could not do anything except turn away from her, stride across the lawn, while in his head the blood drummed like a hammer in his skull.

He thought he heard her cry out, call out his name,

that same note of urgency in it, but he would not hear it. Would not—and could not. Could only reach the driveway, throw himself into his car. Gun the engine to hear it roar, deafening the roaring in his head. And accelerate away…away, away.

But in his head only one question echoed—pounded him.

What kind of woman keeps a child from its father?

The answer tolled in his head like a death knell—the death knell of all his hopes, all his longings.

No woman *he* could ever love.

CHAPTER TEN

SOMEHOW ELOISE SANK back onto the swing seat, her whole body shaking, trembling. How long she sat there, she didn't know. Time had stopped. Life had stopped. Everything had stopped.

Unconsciously, she slid her hand across her abdomen, feeling the telltale swell that had revealed the truth to Vito. A choke broke in her throat. Oh, God, this was supposed to have been the moment their future was sealed by the knowledge that their union was indissoluble, that they would be there for each other for ever! For each other— and for their child...

Telling him was going to be the most wonderful moment of all! The moment I declared how absolutely I trusted him, how absolutely I wanted to make my life with him!

Instead...

The choke came again, and then another, and then a sob, and then she was breaking into pieces, with sobs forcing themselves up through her stricken throat, her whole body shaking and trembling, her hands cramming into her mouth, the tears scalding in her eyes as convulsions of weeping overcame her.

They possessed her utterly, allowing nothing else in—no other emotion other than the final devastation of her hopes. It was like that nightmare day in Rome—but worse... Oh, so much worse!

As the wild sobbing finally ebbed, and there were no more tears to shed, her body exhausted, she wrapped her arms around herself as if to hold herself together. Dully, she realised she could not, *must* not, go on sitting there as shadows lengthened over the pool.

With agonising slowness she got to her feet, her eyes lighting on the champagne bottle, mocking her. A smothered cry broke from her.

She made her way indoors, having piled the coffee cups on to the tray, and headed for the kitchens. Maria would still be upstairs with Johnny.

But when she got indoors it was to find Maria and Johnny busy baking. Johnny rushed to her, telling her he was making brownies for them all, but her smile at him was wan, and she was burningly conscious that Maria's eyes were sharp with concern on her.

'Signor Viscari?' Maria ventured.

'He had to get back to New York. An unexpected call—' Eloise just managed to get the words out.

But Maria was not deceived, Eloise knew, and she shook her head in sorrow, with worry and anxiety open in her face.

All Eloise could do was wait until the brownies were in the oven, then take Johnny upstairs.

'But I want to go in the Ferrari!' he wailed.

'Vito's gone, Johnny,' Eloise said, and the words tolled in her heart.

Desolation filled her. Vito had talked of marriage— but what marriage could there be with him now, filled with anger at her? Only hours earlier she had dreamt of her happily-ever-after ending—of Vito declaring himself to her, and she to him, and then her crowning their happiness, their union, with what she had longed so much to tell him: that they were already blessed with the fruit of that union that was to be for all their lives.

Impossible now! Impossible to contemplate marrying him when his reaction to her pregnancy had been horror!

I can't—I won't marry him like that! It would be a disaster—as disastrous as my parents' marriage was! It would be impossible to do the same!

Round and round the words went in her head, round and round as she somehow got through the rituals of looking after a fretful, fractious Johnny, urged a reluctant Maria to go on her customary visit with her husband to their daughter. For she longed only to have the house to herself, to see Johnny to bed and then head to her own quarters, numb with misery.

As she lay in her bed, sleepless, staring sightlessly at the ceiling, her hand rested on her abdomen. Anguish filled her. Filled every cell in her body. After all her hopes and dreams of Vito to have got it so, so wrong...

Just as I got it wrong in Rome.

She stilled, her eyes distending suddenly. The words had come into her head without volition, without realisation. But now they hung like a burning brand in her consciousness.

She felt her heart leap. She *had* got it wrong in Rome— got it totally, completely wrong! She had totally misunderstood Vito's behaviour there.

What if I'm doing it again now? What if I'm making exactly the same mistake? Ruining everything with my own assumptions!

Urgently she tried to replay in her head that hideous scene by the poolside, when all her hopes and dreams of happily-ever-after had come crashing down around her in the bomb blast of Vito's fury at her. Desperately she tried to remember what he'd said—the words beneath the anger.

'What kind of woman keeps a child from its father?'

That was what Vito had hurled at her! His final condemnation of her. Never giving her time to answer. Never giving her a chance to explain before storming off.

Because the answer she had been desperate to give then was the one that had haunted her from the moment she had discovered she was pregnant. An answer whose roots went back all her life, to the festering pain of her own rejection by her father.

A woman who fears the same rejection now of the child she carries.

It was *that* that had silenced her ever since Vito had found her here in America. That had made her so wary, so scared of telling him what their affair had resulted in.

And that's what I have to tell him—I have to!

She felt her pulse surge again, new emotion filling her overriding the despair and desolation that had consumed her till this moment. Resolution flowed into her. She would *not* give up on Vito! She would not! She wouldn't let his anger with her be the final nail in the coffin of her hopes and dreams.

As the sleepless hours passed her resolve and courage strengthened. She had got it wrong with Vito before, misjudging him for his apparent engagement to his stepcousin. And she had got it wrong now...so catastrophically wrong. Bringing down his anger on her head.

But when I went to him before I made it right! So maybe... Oh, maybe...

If she went to him again would he listen to her? She did not know—could not know. Could know only that for the sake of her chance at happiness she had to make the attempt. Far too much was at stake for her not to do so.

Vito stared out of his hotel room window, looking at the tops of the trees in the green oasis that was Central Park visible. Memory assailed him of how he had stood there by night, so short a time ago, when Eloise had come to him at the hotel to tell him how she had misjudged him, misunderstood him. How they had made their peace after such bitter discord and distrust. How hope had flared within him once again.

But all hope was gone now. Dashed and destroyed. She was not the woman he had thought her to be. She had been hiding from him—day after day after day—the most important thing of all.

How could she do it? How could she talk to me, smile at me, laugh with me—let me kiss her!—and all along know she was carrying our child! She knew it and did not tell me!

Cold ran through him like an icy sluice. How close he'd come to marrying Carla! A hair's breadth! Right now, at this very moment, had he not found the strength of mind to refuse to do so, to walk away from his devil's bargain with her and her mother, he might be married to her! In total ignorance that here in America a child had been conceived—a child who would be born while he was still locked in that unholy marriage, waiting for the annulment he had insisted they must seek once Carla's injured pride and wounded heart had been soothed with their sham marriage.

More memory assailed him—how Eloise had refused to listen to him when he'd found her at the Carldons'—how only a chance word from her employer about how disastrous the loss of Guido's shares had been had brought her to him to make her peace. His face contorted. And still she had not told him she was pregnant with their child! Still she had kept it secret from him!

Emotion seared through him—as it had done over and over again since that moment when his hand had shaped the swell of her abdomen, revealing her condition.

What kind of woman keeps a child from its father?

That was his condemnation of her and it lashed him

over and over again. And that condemnation was like a sword stabbing at *him* too. For it destroyed all that he had let himself hope for—all that he had dreamt of recovering, renewing, discovering with Eloise. His Eloise.

But she isn't that woman! She isn't the woman I thought she was.

All that could ever be between them now was the empty formality of a marriage—as sham, surely, as the one he'd contemplated making with Carla.

The bitterness of it mocked him.

The ringing of the phone penetrated his angry, stricken thoughts. In rapid strides he snatched it up. It would be the front desk, telling him that the hotel limousine was here to take him to the airport. He was flying back to Rome to tell his mother, to bring her here not for a joyous wedding, but for a joyless one—one that would legally unite him to Eloise so that their child would be born within wedlock.

His mind sheered away—it was too painful to contemplate so grim an event.

A moment later he had stilled. It *had* been the front desk—but not for the reason he'd assumed. Slowly, he replaced the handset. A sense of *déjà vu* came over him.

Eloise had come to the hotel.

His expression tightened. What could she possibly say to him now?

After what she had done, what could she possibly say?

Eloise could feel her heart thumping like a sledgehammer inside her as the elevator swept her up to the penthouse floor. Instinctively her hand went to her abdomen, splaying over the swell of her body. The period of nausea had long passed now, and she was glad of it. But for all that there was a churning in her stomach. Nerves stretched taut as wire at what she was facing.

I have to try—I have to try!

Yet as Vito opened the door to her, stepping back to let her in, she could feel her heart plummet. His face was closed—as shuttered as a locked door.

'You wanted to see me.'

His voice was unemotional. The statement devoid of anything to give her hope.

She swallowed, nodded. Crossed to the window opposite, then turned. Deliberately—unlike all the other times she'd met with him here in America—she was wearing a tight-fitting stretch top that moulded her body, revealing totally what she had so assiduously sought to keep concealed from him. Now she flaunted it, lifting her chin as she prepared to speak. Seeking the courage she must find.

She saw his eyes go to her body, cling to the rounded contour. Saw a sudden flash in his expressionless eyes. But *what* had flashed there? Anger? Or something else?

She had to find the words she must say, hard and halting though they would be. So much depended on them. *Everything* depended on them.

Before I was so cautious—so scared of him finding out before I was ready to tell him! But now—now caution is my enemy.

'Vito, I have to talk to you—I *have* to!' The words blurted from her.

He looked at her. 'Do you? I see no necessity for that. The only necessity is for us to arrange our immediate marriage. To legitimise the child you carry.'

His voice was cool, with no emotion in it. But when she had walked into his suite emotion had seared within him. Pain like none he had known. A double blow. Not just because his eyes had lit upon her again, seeing her pale hair drawn back, the fine bones of her face needing no make-up to announce her beauty to him, but because now, for the first time, he could see the state of her pregnancy—her thickening figure, the five-month swell of the child she carried.

Our child.

She had paled at his words, a sickly pallor bleaching her skin.

'Vito—*please!*' The words came from her faintly. 'Please! Hear me out! I beg you! Before...' Her voice trembled. 'Before—when it was you coming to me, when you'd found me here in New York—I refused to listen to you! But please don't do to me what I did to you! Give me a chance—a chance to...to explain...'

Her voice trailed off. She felt herself sway, tension racking her, blood draining from her.

'May...may I sit down?'

She did not wait for an answer, only lowered herself to a sofa, feeling her head clear. Her hands were clutching her bag, as if for dear life, and she held it on her knees, against the swell of her body. Her fingers touched the material stretching across her abdomen, beneath which her precious, precious child was cradled. Whose whole future was at stake now, at this very moment.

It gave her renewed courage to speak. She lifted her face to Vito, across the gaping space between them. Still he had that shuttered look on his face, closing her out. Rejecting her...

'What is there to explain?' he said. 'Your actions have said it all. You are not the woman I thought you were—how could you be, to do what you did?'

The faintness drummed at her again, but she forced herself on. So much depended on what she said.

I kept silent too long—now I must speak.

Her mouth was dry, her throat constricted, but she knew she must force the words from her. Inside, she could feel her heart slugging with hard, heavy beats, could feel acid in her stomach. Every muscle in her body felt weary, exhausted.

After her long, sleepless, fretful night, she'd risen early, finding Maria in the kitchen, begging her to look after Johnny until his parents returned. Then she'd travelled in by train to Manhattan. En route, she had phoned her mother's apartment to ask if she might call by later. The call had gone to voicemail, so she had simply said, her voice strained, that she might need a good lawyer soon.

Because to marry Vito with him thinking so ill of her, looking at her as he was doing now, with his closed, shuttered face, unforgiving, unrelenting, would be impossible—just impossible! All that would be left to her would be some kind of painful, agonising sharing of their child...

Unless...

Once again resolution seared within her. She had to try and win him back—she had to try and recover what her secrecy had cost her. Make good the ill she had done. Too much was at stake for her not to. Far too much.

'So, what is it you want to say?' Vito was demanding, as still she did not speak. 'And what can you possibly say that will change anything?'

His voice was terse, inexpressive, condemning her unheard, condemning her for her deed alone. Not for its cause.

'Vito, I... I want to try and make you understand why I did not tell you I was pregnant.'

She took a hectic breath, then went on, trying to keep her voice steady, to quell the emotions bucketing within her.

'At first, when I discovered it, I was simply in shock—unable to believe it. Through my mother's contacts I'd been offered the position at the Carldons', and of course I had to explain to them the change in my circumstances.

They've been wonderful—even offered to let me continue working after the baby is born if I want. My mother too...' Unconsciously her voice became guarded. 'She has been completely supportive, and I am very appreciative of that. But it was *because* of my mother that I...that I never got in touch with you.'

A frown furrowed Vito's face and his dark gaze transfixed her. She wished he would sit down, for he seemed to be towering over her, brooding and overpowering. It hurt to have him like this, so condemning of her, when before he had been so eager for her.

I have lost his favour and I never knew how much I valued it—how much I took his wanting me for granted.

'How so?' Vito's question was grating, his frown deepening.

She swallowed again, nails pressing into her palms. Forced herself to continue.

'I've never told you anything much about my family— my childhood. About my mother, even. But now I have to.'

She took another breath, forcing herself on, despite the stoniness of Vito's expression.

'When...when my mother was young—my age—she fell in love...hopelessly in love...with my father. They had a whirlwind romance, got married only a handful of months after meeting, swept away on a tide of passion. They thought they would be blissfully happy for ever!'

She heard bitterness creep into her voice. It was still there as she continued.

'But there was nothing happy-ever-after about it at all. It was a classic case of "Marry in haste, repent at leisure." They proved entirely unsuited. My mother was a career woman; my father wanted a traditional wife. And...' she swallowed again '...he wanted a large family. With lots of sons.'

Her voice thinned.

'My mother was not maternal. *Is* not maternal. When I was born she told my father outright that she wasn't going to get pregnant again, would have no more children. Would not give him the sons he craved.'

Her troubled gaze slid past Vito, out of the window, across the expanse of Central Park and the cityscape beyond. Out into the fatherless wasteland of her own childhood.

'So he left her. He left the UK, went to Australia, got himself a divorce and married again. This time around to a woman who was prepared to stay at home and cook his dinner and raise a large family. Which she did. All boys.'

Her gaze came back to Vito. Not seeing him. Seeing a man she had never known. Never would know. Who had not wanted her. Who had rejected her from the moment of her birth.

Her mouth was dry as sand as she spoke again. 'I've never seen him—my father—not since I was a baby. If he walked past me in the street I would not know him. He would be—*is*—a complete stranger to me. He refused all contact with me. Wrote me out of his life as though I did not exist. And, for him, I *don't* exist. I was a girl, and he wasn't interested.'

She gave a little shrug.

'My mother let him go—in the end was glad he went, for it freed her to work as she wanted to. With the help of nannies and au pairs and boarding school she raised me in what spare time she had. Which wasn't much.'

She shrugged again.

'She's always ensured I was well looked after—just not by her. And in her own way,' she acknowledged with painful honesty, 'she loves me, and I her, but it's never been a...a close relationship.'

She got to her feet. Restless suddenly. She paced up and down, trying to find the words she needed to say now.

Vito was not moving. Only his eyes traced her steps. She paused suddenly, looked at him, chin lifting, eyes focusing on him.

'Because of my father, Vito—because of his absolute and utter lack of interest in my existence—when I discovered I was pregnant the first thing I thought of was him. I realised that there were terrible echoes in my situation to my parents'.

He started, his expression changing. 'I am *nothing* like your father!'

She threw up her hands, eyes widening. 'Vito, as far as I knew you were *marrying* another woman—even *before* our child was born! *That* was the truth of what I was facing when I realised I was pregnant!'

Her words seemed only to incense him. His dark eyes flashed with anger.

'*Por Dio*, do you really think I would have married Carla—would even have consented to the farce of our engagement—had I known you were pregnant? That—*that* is what appals me so much, Eloise. That because I didn't know I might actually have married Carla! I might now be married to another woman! The thought of it freezes my blood!'

She reeled from his accusation, but she fought back. She had to fight back.

'But I didn't know that, Vito! To my face you told me you were engaged to Carla! How should I have known it for a lie?'

'I tried to tell you.' His voice was harsh. 'You refused to let me.'

She blanched. Closed her eyes for a moment as if to acknowledge the justice of his accusation. Then she opened them again to acknowledge it.

'Yes, I know—and I have had my punishment, have I not? Had I not fled Rome—'

She broke off. What use to go over that again? None. It was gone now. It was the future that counted—that she had to try and save.

'But I *did* flee Rome. And I faced, here, a future without you. A future as a single mother—as my own mother is. Vito—what else could I have done? You were engaged to another woman—would be marrying her, I assumed. To have informed you that I was pregnant would have achieved nothing!'

She saw him move as if to speak again and stumbled on, desperate to make him understand why she had kept silent.

'Vito, even if...even if you had not married Carla because I'd told you I was pregnant, and you'd married me instead—even setting aside all the dreadful complications of the Viscari shares—how could I *possibly* want a husband who'd *had* to marry me? Not married me out of choice! Not because he'd *wanted* to marry me! But simply to legitimise a child he'd never intended to conceive and never wanted in the first place! When all you'd wanted— all I *knew* you wanted, because of that nightmare scene in Rome, when Carla stormed in on us—was to marry *her*, not me! Just what kind of marriage would that have been, Vito? What kind of husband would you have been? What kind of father would you have made, forced into it unwillingly?'

Again she saw him try and interrupt her, but she would not let him. She ploughed on. She had to say this—say it all. Bitter and hard though it was.

'I wrote you off, Vito. I had to. It was all I could do. I had to face the future on my own—just as my mother had to. Only when you tracked me down—and only when I realised just what you had been through with Carla, and the loss of half your heritage—did I know that I must re-evaluate my decision.'

She rubbed a weary hand across her brow.

'And that is what I did, Vito. From the moment you said, "No pressure", that is what I did. Hour by hour, day by day.'

She looked at him with infinite sorrow and sadness in her eyes, in her voice.

'As you wooed me again, courting me again with every glance, every smile, everything started growing again between us. And I started to hope—oh, Vito, I started to *hope*! When you told me it was not the past you were seeking to recapture but our future together—then I knew that everything was changing for ever.'

Her expression changed, her face working.

'But would it be enough, Vito? That is what I wanted to know! My parents were romantically in love—but their utterly opposing views on children severed them completely! What if we were the same? What if the child that I want so much—so rejoice in bearing, that's so absolutely precious to me—what if that was the very, very last thing you wanted? What if, instead of uniting us, our child divided us?'

She shook her head, all the fears that had racked her open in her face. Her voice dropped.

'How would I know that you would not be like my father? That was what haunted me! I *had* to know you would not be like him before I entrusted you with the knowledge of our child—before I entrusted my life to you! *Our* lives to you! I *had* to get it right, Vito! I'd got it wrong about you *twice* before! First I was weaving dreams about you while we were in Europe, wondering if you were The One! Only to crash and burn hideously when Carla appeared! And then—dear God...'

She rubbed a weary hand across her forehead. 'I got it wrong again—disastrously—over Carla and your uncle's shares! So I could not, just *could not*, risk making a third mistake over you! Not when our child's happiness would be at stake.'

She paused, her expression changing. Softening.

'It was when I saw you with little Johnny. When I saw how easily you spoke to him, how natural you were with him, how patient, how you so obviously liked him...' She gave a little choking laugh. 'And yesterday—all that time playing with him, paying him attention, enjoying his company...'

She swallowed.

'It confirmed to me everything I'd come to believe about you, made me trust in you. Trust that you would always be a good father to our own child. So then I knew— I finally knew—that the time had come when it was safe to tell you, knowing you would welcome the news, rejoice at it.'

She fell silent. Then lifted her eyes to him, her face contorting.

'Instead—'

Her hand pressed against her mouth. Vito had not moved—not a muscle. He stood as immobile as a statue, his face as closed, as shuttered as it had ever been. Rejecting her. Rejecting what she was telling him. Rejecting her plea for understanding.

'Instead,' she said dully, heaviness weighing her down, crushing her with a sense of hopelessness, 'you reacted in horror. You were appalled to discover I was pregnant. And every fear I possessed was proved right.'

She fell silent. She had said it all.

For an endless moment the silence stretched. Then Vito spoke.

'I was appalled at your *secrecy*, Eloise. Not your pregnancy.'

His voice was remote, as if coming from a long, long way away.

'*That's* what I condemned,' he said.

The silence came again—longer now. Unbearable. Faintness was drumming at her again, but she had to speak, to ask one last question. The only question in the universe.

'And do you still condemn me, Vito, after hearing why I kept it secret from you?'

She saw him take a breath, saw his chest rise, heard the sharpness of its intake.

'I don't know,' he said.

Abruptly he turned away, pacing across the room. A million thoughts were in his head...a million emotions burned through him. Jangled and tangled, jarring and marring. Making no sense.

He halted, looked back at her. 'What do you want, Eloise?'

There was only neutrality in his voice, but it was deceptive. She started as he said it, looking at him warily.

'What do I want?'

She heard her own voice echo his. Heard it again in her heart. What *did* she want?

Her own thoughts answered her.

I want my happy-ever-after. The one I've longed for all my life. My determination from a child has been to find the right man, fall in love, make a family. Live happily ever after.

But were such things even possible? When Vito had first swept her away she'd wondered if it had meant that he was 'The One'. Then she'd crashed and burned in Rome, over Carla and those shares. Then here, in America, it had seemed to be within her reach again. Then, yesterday, she had crashed and burned again.

And now—

New thoughts came.

Maybe what I've longed for all my life is just a dream—

a dream I dreamt because I wanted to recreate my parents' marriage as it should have been, so I could have the childhood I craved. Maybe that's why I clung to that dream.

She let her eyes rest on Vito. She had been through so much on his account—happiness and bliss. Despair and rejection. Hope and fear.

But of all those emotions, clashing and contradictory, what was the one emotion that remained?

She knew its name. Knew it because it was the emotion that leapt in her every time her hand shaped her body, cradled the life growing within.

But if that was not what Vito felt she must not name it. *Coward!*

The word stabbed at her, shocking her.

More words came, forced their way in.

You don't dare tell him because you fear his rejection! It was his rejection in Rome that slayed you! His rejection yesterday that did the same! But Vito isn't your father! So tell him—tell him now what it is you want!

She looked at him again, so short a distance away. Their lives would be linked for ever now, because of the child she carried. They were bound indissolubly because of that.

And for one reason more. A reason that would bind her to him all her life.

Slowly she spoke, never taking her eyes from him. Declaring everything.

'I want, Vito, you to love me and our child as I love *you* and our child. That is all I want,' she said. 'All I will ever want.'

Her eyes dipped. What would he say? How would he reply? She could not see his face, with her eyes lowered, but she heard his voice. It was strange...so strange.

'All my life,' he said slowly, in that strange new voice,

'I have wanted to find a woman I would love as dearly as my father loved my mother. Their marriage, to me, seemed all that marriage should ever be! And when I lost my father it was...unbearable. It still is, Eloise. Every day I miss him, grown man though I am. A father is for life—'

He broke off, and her eyes lifted, going instantly to his face, where emotion shadowed his eyes.

Then the shadow lifted. 'Eloise, *that* is why I was so harsh with you! I couldn't bear to think that you might have taken our child from me! That you might have thought a child did not need its father—'

'But I don't! Vito—that's why I feared to tell you! I couldn't have borne it if you'd rejected our child as my father rejected me!'

Her voice was a cry.

'Never! As God is my witness, *never* will I reject our child—and never, Eloise...oh, Eloise...never will I reject *you*!'

He came towards her, caught her hands. Emotion was pouring through him, a tidal wave.

'Do you mean it? What you said? That you want only my love?'

She lifted her face to his. Tears swam in her eyes.

'Yes! Oh, yes! But only...' the shadow was there in her eyes again '...only if you love me...'

Her answer was a kiss. As swift, as swooping as a summer swallow, silencing her doubts.

'If you had told me even a second before I found out I would have embraced you as I do now!'

As he spoke from his overflowing heart his arms came around her, holding her close, so close against him.

'Oh, Eloise, my Eloise, my precious, beloved Eloise—how could you think I would not cherish a child between us? I understand your fears—now that I know them—but you never had need of them! Not for an instant!'

A breath shuddered through him and he held her a little away from him now, so he could speak to her. His gaze poured into her.

'It was *my* fears, Eloise, that made me condemn you. The thought of what might have been... To have had a child growing up here, away from me, unknown to me, kept from me by the very woman I had fallen in love with.'

Her face worked. 'If I'd only spoken earlier...'

He shook his head. 'If I had only let you speak—let you explain your secrecy...'

She swallowed. 'And if I had let you speak in Rome—let you explain about Carla, about everything...'

He gave a shaky laugh. They had come so close to losing each other. To losing what was most precious between them.

'Never again!' he breathed. 'From this day onward, my beloved, we shall always, *always* hear each other out! About everything!'

Her answering smile was wavering, and tears still weighed on her lashes. But inside her huge, sweeping emotions were lifting her high. Joy was lighting within her...happiness was soaring. And then the tears suddenly cascaded down, shedding their burden. Her face convulsed.

'Eloise!'

Alarm was in his voice and he wrapped her to him again, enveloping her as sobs broke from her.

So many emotions—so many hopes, so many fears, so many dreams. And now those dreams had come true. Vito was hers, and she was his, and their child was theirs for ever...

He let her weep, let all the emotions spill out of her, echoing the tumult draining from him too as he cradled her in his arms, murmuring in his own language to her, words and fragments of words that held a lifetime's love in them.

And when at last her tears were shed, and a wondrous peace eased into her, a shining joy filled her to the brim, his hands gently lifted her face away from where it was buried in his shoulder.

His eyes were soft and filled with a tenderness that caught at all her senses. His kiss was as gentle as a summer's breeze, as true as the love between them. Happiness filled her.

As he drew back his eyes held hers, entwining with hers. 'How blessed I am,' he said. 'To have you and our child to be born.'

'As blessed as I am,' she echoed, her face softening with love. 'To have you and...' She paused, then smiled as she spoke on. 'And our son to be born.'

Vito stilled. 'Son? You *know*?'

She nodded, drawing a little back from him, nodding. Smiling. So joyous to be telling him.

'I had early tests done, because I was anxious to know all was well, and they asked if I wanted to know the baby's gender. I said yes, because I'm never one to bear suspense!' She gave half a laugh, then smiled again. 'And because I knew Johnny would ask once he realised I was having a baby, once I'd started to show.'

She paused a moment, her expression changing.

'Vito—what was your father's name?'

The question hung in the air, heavy with portent. He knew why she had asked, and he loved her the more for it.

'Enrico,' he answered. There was the slightest choke in his voice.

'Enrico...' Eloise echoed, with the same musing smile playing around her lips. 'Would Rico be the diminutive form, do you think? Suitable for a baby?'

Vito's long lashes swept down. 'Entirely suitable,' he

said. His hand slid over her abdomen, and there was a look of wonder on his face. 'Little Rico,' he murmured.

'Little Rico,' she echoed tenderly.

He kissed her again—gently, softly—his hand resting where it was. Family already...as they would always be.

The jarring ring of the phone startled them, and with an exclamation Vito relinquished her to answer it.

He listened, then frowned. 'We have a visitor in the lobby,' he announced. 'She wishes to speak to you.'

Eloise frowned, too, then came to the phone.

'*Mum?*' she said incredulously.

Her mother's crisp tones penetrated even to Vito.

'I came the moment I got your voicemail. Eloise, what on earth is happening? The last I heard was that you'd decided to accept this man after all! So why this talk of custody challenges?'

With difficulty, Eloise cut across her mother. 'Mum— ignore that! It's all right after all—it's all right! In fact...' she gave a laugh of pure emotion '...it's wonderful! Just *wonderful*! Mum—'

But the line had gone dead. Slowly she replaced the receiver. Glanced at Vito.

'That was my mother,' she said unnecessarily. 'And I have a bad feeling that she may be about to make an appearance.'

There was foreboding in her voice, but Vito only smiled reassuringly. 'It is time I made her acquaintance,' he said.

Eloise made a face. 'She can be very...formidable,' she said cautiously.

'I shall be prepared,' Vito said resolutely. 'And I shall take pains to assure her that I will be *nothing* like your father! If you wish to make a glittering career for yourself you are *entirely* free to do so—though of course, as a nanny, I would hope that your first devotion would be to our child. And perhaps,' he added tentatively, 'to our other children, if that is a happy proposition for you? But of course if not—'

She did not hesitate to reassure him. 'Oh, Vito, as many as we want!'

A rap on the door interrupted this exchange, and Vito crossed with long strides to answer it.

The woman who sailed in was severely dressed in a sharply cut navy suit, with immaculate hair and a brisk manner. She stopped short, her eyes raking Vito. Then she went to her daughter.

'Would either of you care to update me?' she said, her English accent accentuating the cut of her question.

'It's all sorted,' Eloise provided. She crossed to Vito, wrapped her arm around his waist. 'It's all wonderful. Fantastic. Blissful!' She gave a sigh of happiness.

Her mother's gimlet eyes surveyed them for a moment longer, as if assessing what she saw. Then, abruptly, she nodded.

'Good,' she said. 'In which case Vito might as well be party to this.'

She sat herself down on the sofa, extracting from her handbag a bulky envelope which she placed on the coffee table. Eloise, a bewildered expression on her face, slid onto the sofa opposite and looked at the envelope. Vito came and sat down beside her, a slight frown of curiosity on his face as Eloise pushed the envelope at him.

'Well, don't just stare at it—open it!' Eloise's mother instructed impatiently.

Her tone of voice changed, and she looked at Vito.

'Eloise will be the first to tell you that I am unlikely to make a doting grandmother—I leave that office to your own mother!—but nevertheless please believe me that I will take my responsibilities to my grandson very seriously. As I trust this demonstrates.'

She nodded at the envelope, which Vito was beginning to open. It yielded a bulky document, which he unfolded and looked down at. Stared at.

Then his eyes flashed upwards. 'I don't understand…'

There was no expression in his voice. Nothing except incomprehension. And shock. Total shock.

Eloise looked up at him, consternation in her eyes. 'Vito, what is it?'

Nervelessly he handed the document to her, but his gaze was still on her mother. He said something in Italian that Eloise did not understand. She stared at the document. It was in legalese, formal and convoluted, but as she gazed, and made herself read it, she felt herself go completely still.

Her eyes, too, flashed up to her mother. 'What *is* this?' she asked. Her voice was like a ghost.

Her mother stood up and looked at them with an expression of complete satisfaction on her face.

'It is, Eloise, exactly what it says it is.' Her voice was as brisk as ever, with a snap of impatience in it directed at her daughter. 'It's a certificate for the shares originally owned by Vito's uncle! Now owned by your son.'

The satisfaction was even more marked now.

'What?' The question exploded like a bullet from Eloise. 'Mum, what have you *done*?'

'Oh, for heaven's sake, Eloise, don't be so obtuse!' The snap was even more marked. 'It's perfectly obvious. I've acquired Marlene Viscari's shareholding.'

Eloise stared—she could do nothing else. But above her she could hear Vito's voice. Sounding hollow. Disbelieving.

'But they were bought by Nic Falcone,' he said.

He swallowed, still staring. Incapable of anything other than disbelief and paralysing shock. What the *hell* was going on here?

'No,' Eloise's mother contradicted him, 'they were bought on his behalf by the hedge fund Nic Falcone had to enlist in order to fund the acquisition. I have now bought them from the hedge fund at a price they did not wish to refuse. Falcone had no say in the matter—though I believe he is not best pleased!'

She snapped her handbag shut with a decisive click.

'However, his displeasure is of no account. The shares are now the property of your son—although,' she said kindly, her gaze sweeping Eloise and Vito, 'the two of you are his proxies until he reaches majority.'

Shock was still detonating through Vito. Shock and incomprehension.

'Mrs Dean,' he said, his voice still hollow, 'I don't understand...'

Eloise's mother held up her hand in an imperious fashion. 'I don't use my married name—when I set up in New York I reverted to my maiden name. Forrester,' she said, with something of a snap. 'I saw no reason to credit my faithless ex with any part of what I had achieved without him!'

Vito's mouth opened. Then closed. Then, from somewhere very, very deep in the recesses of his brain, a synapse fired.

He stared at Eloise's mother. 'Forrester...' he said.

He paused. Another synapse fired, giving him a possible explanation of what he'd just heard.

'Good God,' he said tonelessly, 'Forrester Travis...'

Disbelief was the only emotion in his voice.

'Oh, for heaven's sake, Eloise!' came her mother's snap. 'Don't tell me you've never explained to him what I do!'

Eloise looked at Vito. 'Mum runs some kind of investment firm,' she said belatedly. 'With a guy called Travis. Somewhere downtown.'

A noise escaped from Vito's throat. 'Your mother is

Susan Forrester?' he said blankly, as if he could not credit his own words. 'Susan Forrester of Forrester Travis.'

He took a breath, his gaze going back to Eloise.

'*Cara mia*, Forrester Travis is one of the world's foremost hedge funds! It has something like thirty billion dollars under investment—'

'Thirty-four point five,' corrected Susan Forrester, one of the most outstandingly influential women on Wall Street. She drew breath. 'Well,' she said dryly, 'if my daughter really never told you about me at least I can be satisfied you haven't made up to her for her prospects!'

Vito got to his feet. Looked at Eloise's mother. His mind was still reeling with who she was and what she had done.

'Thank you,' he said quietly. 'Thank you from the bottom of my heart.'

'It was the least I could do,' said Eloise's mother. Her expression changed again, and she sighed. 'I told you I won't make a doting grandmother, but whatever Eloise says about me I want only her happiness.'

There was the slightest catch in her voice, and then she squared her shoulders.

'Well, now that everything is sorted I must go. I'm lunching with the president of Banco Brasilão, and clearly...' her voice became dry '... I am quite unnecessary here.'

Her voice became even more dry.

'Vito will need time to assimilate the situation, and doubtless to phone Italy and apprise his own mother of her forthcoming welcome transformation into a grandmother! I look forward to making her acquaintance in due course, and to reaching some degree of mutual agreement as to the style of wedding you two are to have.'

Eloise leant forward to catch her mother's hand. 'Mum,' she said, and her voice was charged with emotion, 'thank you.' She swallowed. '*Thank* you,' she said again. 'For everything.'

She couldn't say any more—her throat was suddenly tight again. She could only press her mother's hand, hoping by that feeble gesture to express her gratitude for what her mother had done—waved her Wall Street wand and restored to Vito the Viscari legacy that Marlene had so ruthlessly disposed of. The legacy that Vito had sacrificed to win her back...the price he had paid for her love.

He gave it up for me! Put aside the vow he made his father for my sake.

And now he had been rewarded for his sacrifice, and she was glad with all her heart and so, *so* grateful to her mother! She felt her eyes mist and knew, with a deep sense of familiar irony, just how much her mother would hate such emotionality.

'Silly girl,' her mother said, but Eloise could hear a difference in her voice from her usual briskness. She patted Eloise's hand and then drew her own back, glancing at her slim gold watch. 'I must go,' she said. 'My car will be waiting.'

The briskness was back in her voice, and in her manner. She held up a hand in farewell and was gone.

Vito turned to Eloise. 'Did I just dream that?' he asked.

Then his eyes went to the documentation on the coffee table. The papers that had restored to him at a stroke what Marlene's machinations had wrenched from his family. He shook his head slowly in wonder. Then another thought occurred to him.

'Your mother talked about a wedding—but...' there was hesitancy in his voice '...is that something you want, *cara mia*?'

She wrapped her arms around his neck. 'Only if you do,' she replied.

His face lit. 'It is my dearest wish!'

His mouth swooped to hers, kissing her tenderly. Then less tenderly. More sensually. At once within Eloise desire quickened, answering his.

Vito paused, though his arms were tight around her. 'If your mother and mine insist on a fancy wedding, it could take a while to organise. So I was thinking...in the meantime perhaps we might pre-empt our honeymoon.'

He smiled wickedly.

'How about testing out the new Viscari Hotel on Ste Cecile?' He grazed her lips with his persuasively. 'Do you think the Carldons would let you disappear for a long weekend?'

Eloise laughed. 'Considering Laura Carldon has been desperate to get us together, I'm sure they will! And if she balks—well, her mother and mine are good friends. That's how I got the job as Johnny's nanny and it might help.'

'Great.' Vito grinned. 'And, speaking of the Carldons, what about if I offer Maria and Giuseppe the pick of the Viscari Hotels collection for an extended holiday? I need to say thank you to them—after all, had it not been for them I would never have found you.'

Eloise's grip on him tightened. The very thought of Vito never finding her....

'Tell me,' Vito was continuing, 'how long do you think the Carldons will need to replace you? That will set the timing of our wedding.'

'A few weeks, I should think. Laura has already mentioned it to me as a possibility. Vito, they must come to the wedding—and Johnny too! Maybe,' she mused, 'he'd like to be our page boy?'

'More likely our chauffeur!' Vito laughed. He swooped another kiss on her mouth. 'Any more wedding details to be finalised right now? Or can we get on with what I've been longing to do for so long?'

She lifted limpid eyes to him. 'What might that be, Vito?'

A wicked smile quivered at her lips. And was answered by his.

'This,' he said.

With a single scoop she was in his arms and he was striding with her into the bedroom, lowering her gently down upon the bed's surface.

'This,' he repeated, and came down beside her. 'This,' he confirmed, and started to make love to her.

Eloise was the woman he loved, the woman who carried the son he already loved, who melded them into the family they would always be.

Always.

CHAPTER ELEVEN

CARIBBEAN MOONLIGHT SHAFTED through the slats of the louvred windows of their room, and the slow beating of the ceiling fan high in the vaulted roof echoed the beating of her heart. Vito led her towards the bed, his fingers entwined with hers, his naked body outlined in all its masculine perfection by the silver light of the slanting moon.

With a little sigh Eloise folded herself down onto the cool surface of the sheets, letting her thighs splay loosely, her moon-silvered hair flow out across the pillows. Displaying herself to Vito.

For a long, timeless moment he gazed down on her.

'How beautiful you are—how entirely beautiful to me...' His voice was a soft, heartfelt murmur.

She trailed a hand softly across her ripening figure.

'Make the most of it,' she said, and smiled. 'Soon I'll be like a barrage balloon!'

'Impossible!'

He shook his head and came down beside her, his hand resting on hers, his mouth lowering to graze the rounded surface below which their precious son was growing, paying homage to his unborn child whose mother he loved so, so much.

Then his mouth lifted from her only to dip again, grazing the valley between the ripened breasts that were cresting for him alone. Desire quickened in him and his thigh moved across hers, his palms cupping her sweet, full breasts.

She gave a little moan in her throat at the sensations he was arousing with his thumbs teasing over the hardened coral peaks. He felt her spine arch, felt her thighs part to let his fall between them, felt her revelling in the sensual pressure it created in her body's core, in the warmth beginning to heat there.

Her hands folded around his back, pressing her to him as her mouth reached for his, wanting more, so much more...

Their kiss was deep, arousing, and he felt his body surge with need, heard her breath quicken and knew his own was quickening too. His kisses deepened, opening her mouth to him even as her body was opening to him as he moved across her fully, one hand sliding to the nape of her neck to lift her head, to arch her body as he slid within.

A gasp of pleasure broke from her as he did so, and one from him as well, as he felt her fullness all around him, felt the delicate tissues of her body engorge, felt the absolute fusion of their two physical beings echoing the absolute fusion of their hearts.

He started to move upon her in the ancient rhythm of the union of male and female, as old as time and as powerful. He felt the passion build within him, within her, between them both, felt her thighs straining against his, her spine arching more. His mouth devoured her urgently, driven by a need so overpowering he could not resist it, could not delay it.

Words broke from him and she heard them through the drumming in her senses, felt the mounting urgency in her own body, flooded now with a supreme need for the fulfilment that she craved. His pace quickened, sending her into vortex after vortex of climbing arousal.

Her hands clutched at his shoulders, nails digging into him, and her body strained against his, moving with hypnotic whorls against him, feeling his possession of her deepen further yet as she lifted to him, took him in more deeply, closed tight around him, clasping him with her whole body, melding their tissues, becoming one single sensual being. One single beating heart.

And then one single tide of ecstasy was flooding across them, making them cry out in unison with a pleasure so intense it was a conflagration of their limbs, their bodies, that went on and on and on...

An eternity later, when time had resumed, and the slow beat of the ceiling fan was marking the seconds yet again, Eloise lay in the cradle of his arms, feeling a peace fill her that was so profound it was as if there had never been anything else in all the world.

Vito smoothed her hair, glorying in the tangled locks spun from finest silk. He smiled at her, his eyes warm with love for her. One arm was around her; the other rested protectively across the swell of their child.

Suddenly his expression in the dim moonlight changed. Became one of wonder.

'Eloise...' His voice was a breath.

Her eyes widened. She knew suddenly what he had felt. What she too had felt. A tiny fluttering within.

'He moved!' Vito's voice was husky. 'I felt him move!'

Her eyes clung to Vito. 'It's the first time—the first time I've felt him move!'

Her own hand moved to her abdomen, beside Vito's.

'Oh, Vito, he's real! He's real—he's real!' Her voice caught. 'I knew from the scans that he was there, but this... Oh, this is him making himself known to us!'

She felt tears of joy prickle in her eyes, heard the catch in Vito's echoing voice.

'Little Rico—our son. Our child.'

He kissed her, tender and fierce at the same time. How blessed he was! Eloise, his child, and all the other blessings rich upon them. The relief of knowing that his family legacy was safe again, that it was already in the possession of his precious son...

Eloise's arms wrapped about him, holding him close against her. Happiness enveloped her. Soon now they would be married. United for ever. Vito's mother would be flying over to start the preparations as soon as she and Vito returned from Ste Cecile.

'She's ecstatic!' Vito had told her. 'She cannot wait to meet you!'

His expression had softened.

'All this has brought joy back into her life, and I know that she will make the most welcoming mother-in-law you could ever wish for.'

He'd given a laugh.

'As well as styling our wedding in New York—with your approval, of course!—she's already planning Rico's christening in Rome!' He'd looked at her. 'Do you think your mother could find time in her schedule to fly to Italy for it?'

'Of course she will!' Eloise had assured him. 'We may be Rico's proxies for the shares, but she'll want to ensure he grows up knowing it was his non-doting grandmother who got them for him!'

'Well, my mother will do double doting, I promise you that!' Vito had laughed again. 'We'll have to make sure she doesn't spoil him.'

Eloise's eyes had softened. 'She can spoil him all she likes,' she'd said. Her eyes had shadowed. 'My only regret is that Rico will have no grandfathers to do likewise.'

'Yes,' he'd said, sadness in his voice. 'In my father he would have had the best grandfather a boy could dream of!' His expression had changed. 'Is there no chance your father might—?'

Eloise had shaken her head, her mouth tight. 'No. If in years to come Rico wants to make contact with his half-cousins, then I will support him in that. But for me...' She'd looked away. 'I won't risk it, Vito. And I don't want it either. He made his choice. He didn't choose me. Not even to stay in touch and send birthday cards. So I won't choose him either.'

She had touched his cheek, her eyes searching. 'Not everything in life is perfect, Vito. You and I both know that—we each have our own deep sorrows. But—' she'd taken a reviving breath '—we also have more than our share of joys!'

He'd kissed her then, in agreement, in reassurance, in love, and now she lay within the cradle of his arms, here on this beautiful tropical island where they would later come back for their real honeymoon, their bodies sated after their desire for each other—a desire that would endure for ever...even through her barrage balloon phase.

Eloise grinned to herself. She knew, without any doubt at all that the greatest joy of all was their love for each other, and for the child waiting to be born into that love.

The sonorous music swelled, lifting upwards to one last crescendo before falling silent. The hushed murmurings of the congregation stilled as the priest raised his hands and began to speak the words of the ancient sacrament in the age-old ceremony.

Inside his breast Vito could feel his heart beating strongly. Emotion filled him—and he turned his head towards the woman now standing at his side.

Gowned in ivory, her face veiled, his bride waited for

him. Waited for him to say the words that would unite them in marriage...join him in marriage to the woman he loved more than life itself.

To Eloise, his beloved bride...

* * * * *

If you enjoyed
CLAIMING HIS SCANDALOUS LOVE-CHILD
why not explore these other stories
by Julia James?

CAPTIVATED BY THE GREEK
A TYCOON TO BE RECKONED WITH
A CINDERELLA FOR THE GREEK

Available now!

MILLS & BOON®
Hardback – November 2017

ROMANCE

The Italian's Christmas Secret	Sharon Kendrick
A Diamond for the Sheikh's Mistress	Abby Green
The Sultan Demands His Heir	Maya Blake
Claiming His Scandalous Love-Child	Julia James
Valdez's Bartered Bride	Rachael Thomas
The Greek's Forbidden Princess	Annie West
Kidnapped for the Tycoon's Baby	Louise Fuller
A Night, A Consequence, A Vow	Angela Bissell
Christmas with Her Millionaire Boss	Barbara Wallace
Snowbound with an Heiress	Jennifer Faye
Newborn Under the Christmas Tree	Sophie Pembroke
His Mistletoe Proposal	Christy McKellen
The Spanish Duke's Holiday Proposal	Robin Gianna
The Rescue Doc's Christmas Miracle	Amalie Berlin
Christmas with Her Daredevil Doc	Kate Hardy
Their Pregnancy Gift	Kate Hardy
A Family Made at Christmas	Scarlet Wilson
Their Mistletoe Baby	Karin Baine
The Texan Takes a Wife	Charlene Sands
Twins for the Billionaire	Sarah M. Anderson

MILLS & BOON®
Large Print – November 2017

ROMANCE

The Pregnant Kavakos Bride	Sharon Kendrick
The Billionaire's Secret Princess	Caitlin Crews
Sicilian's Baby of Shame	Carol Marinelli
The Secret Kept from the Greek	Susan Stephens
A Ring to Secure His Crown	Kim Lawrence
Wedding Night with Her Enemy	Melanie Milburne
Salazar's One-Night Heir	Jennifer Hayward
The Mysterious Italian Houseguest	Scarlet Wilson
Bound to Her Greek Billionaire	Rebecca Winters
Their Baby Surprise	Katrina Cudmore
The Marriage of Inconvenience	Nina Singh

HISTORICAL

Ruined by the Reckless Viscount	Sophia James
Cinderella and the Duke	Janice Preston
A Warriner to Rescue Her	Virginia Heath
Forbidden Night with the Warrior	Michelle Willingham
The Foundling Bride	Helen Dickson

MEDICAL

Mummy, Nurse...Duchess?	Kate Hardy
Falling for the Foster Mum	Karin Baine
The Doctor and the Princess	Scarlet Wilson
Miracle for the Neurosurgeon	Lynne Marshall
English Rose for the Sicilian Doc	Annie Claydon
Engaged to the Doctor Sheikh	Meredith Webber

MILLS & BOON®
Hardback – December 2017

ROMANCE

His Queen by Desert Decree	Lynne Graham
A Christmas Bride for the King	Abby Green
Captive for the Sheikh's Pleasure	Carol Marinelli
Legacy of His Revenge	Cathy Williams
A Night of Royal Consequences	Susan Stephens
Carrying His Scandalous Heir	Julia James
Christmas at the Tycoon's Command	Jennifer Hayward
Innocent in the Billionaire's Bed	Clare Connelly
Snowed in with the Reluctant Tycoon	Nina Singh
The Magnate's Holiday Proposal	Rebecca Winters
The Billionaire's Christmas Baby	Marion Lennox
Christmas Bride for the Boss	Kate Hardy
Christmas with the Best Man	Susan Carlisle
Navy Doc on Her Christmas List	Amy Ruttan
Christmas Bride for the Sheikh	Carol Marinelli
Her Knight Under the Mistletoe	Annie O'Neil
The Nurse's Special Delivery	Louisa George
Her New Year Baby Surprise	Sue MacKay
His Secret Son	Brenda Jackson
Best Man Under the Mistletoe	Jules Bennett

MILLS & BOON®
Large Print – November 2017

ROMANCE

An Heir Made in the Marriage Bed	Anne Mather
The Prince's Stolen Virgin	Maisey Yates
Protecting His Defiant Innocent	Michelle Smart
Pregnant at Acosta's Demand	Maya Blake
The Secret He Must Claim	Chantelle Shaw
Carrying the Spaniard's Child	Jennie Lucas
A Ring for the Greek's Baby	Melanie Milburne
The Runaway Bride and the Billionaire	Kate Hardy
The Boss's Fake Fiancée	Susan Meier
The Millionaire's Redemption	Therese Beharrie
Captivated by the Enigmatic Tycoon	Bella Bucannon

HISTORICAL

Marrying His Cinderella Countess	Louise Allen
A Ring for the Pregnant Debutante	Laura Martin
The Governess Heiress	Elizabeth Beacon
The Warrior's Damsel in Distress	Meriel Fuller
The Knight's Scarred Maiden	Nicole Locke

MEDICAL

Healing the Sheikh's Heart	Annie O'Neil
A Life-Saving Reunion	Alison Roberts
The Surgeon's Cinderella	Susan Carlisle
Saved by Doctor Dreamy	Dianne Drake
Pregnant with the Boss's Baby	Sue MacKay
Reunited with His Runaway Doc	Lucy Clark